SHOULD I....
FALL IN LOVE

BY

SHRADHA KHANNA

RIGI PUBLICATION

SHOULD I... FALL IN LOVE

By

SHRADHA KHANNA

Copyright©SHRADHA KHANNA 2016

Originally published in India

ISBN: 978-93-84314-04-0

Published by RIGI PUBLICATION

777, Street no.9, Krishna Nagar
Khanna-141401 (Punjab), India
Website: www.rigipublication.com
Email: info@rigipublication.com
Phone: +91-9357710014, +91-9465468291

Dedication

To Avneet Kaur,

With love and gratitude

Also, thanks to the infinite support Sucheta Khanna (mom), Rajnesh Khanna (dad), Vishwas Khanna, Chhavi P. Sehgal, Akanksha Ralli Arora, Richal Manchanda, Shria kaur, Darshpreet Singh Khera, Garima Arora, Kunal Arora, Sandeep khera, Shifaali Khanna, Dilmohan Singh Sidana, Manish Madan, Ankit Singhal.

Thank you for keeping with my stupidities, for encouraging me with my weird ideas, for inspiring me and believing in my characters.

"We don't meet people by mere accident
but they are meant to cross our paths for
a reason." – Unknown

CHAPTER 1

Sitting with a bunch of friends on Saturday night, forces me to think what I would be without them. I have known them for all my life & they have been my strength of pillar. When I look back through the 29 years of my life, my goof-ups, the guys I date, my spirituality phase and then back to the clubbing phase - they have been there watching out for me, giving me their shoulders to cry and being blunt about their thoughts about me. Still, sometimes I am awed & surprised for their existence in my life. Lost in my thoughts, suddenly Shania, my childhood bestie shouts from the bar-"Which mocktail do you want?", "The usual" I told her.

Sometimes I feel envious and sometimes even proud to see Shania & Rahul together. They have been married for two years now theirs was an arranged marriage but somehow it never looks like one. The cliché "Love at first sight" is what happened with them. My eyes simply look around the bar checking out the crowd but no one seems to be up to the mark. Some guys are busy ogling the petite girls and some are too drunk to know what's happening around. Sometimes I think that, if marriages are made in heaven, my guy, I think drank too much to show up at the altar, if there is any who exists in heaven.

I should be happy, as there is good music and my favourite band playing but nope my mind is somewhere else today. My mind is still stuck on the idea what went wrong with me? Why I am alone in this huge world where millions of guy's exist? Where is the one, if he really exists, I suppose and why is he taking so much time to come? I know I am in a brooding state today but then it happens when all your friends are married, dancing with their spouses & you sitting alone just staring at them and wishing if was you.

Sandy notices me voices out his concern, "You know just brooding here making faces would not get you anywhere. You should come

& dance with us after all you are the lucky unmarried one among us". "Yes, that definitely does make me feel better". We laughed it off & I am on the floor, flirting with my friends, enjoying the good music as this feeling somehow just does not leave me alone. So, I decided I would deal with this brooding tomorrow; tonight I let my self be free & flirtatious. After all, it is my twenty-ninth birthday party.

CHAPTER 2

I really do not know when I crashed in my apartment, but it was one of the most magical nights in my life. Somehow, it just turned out right. My feet were aching from dancing. I just needed a body message. My phone beeped, it is a message from my boss, I forgot that today was his house warming party & I promised to bake him my favourite cake. How much I hate when my Sunday mornings are disturbed with these out of the way gestures I make to people just to please them.

Finally, with much motivation I steal myself from the warmth of my bed & look out for the things needed for the cake. I called my boss, hyper as he is he started shouting on the phone "When are you going to bring your lazy ass to my party?" As cool as I can be "boss chill, I am just baking your favourite cake, as soon as it is baked, I will be there entertaining your favourite people." "Fine, one hour all you have", he screamed. The same old threat - "Okay boss." How many times I have listened to same old lines from him & he knows it would not affect me in any way possible. Still, keeping the cake in oven, I went for a shower. Deciding for an outfit for house warming parties has always been a task for me. Should I wear something light & floral or something more on the sexy & ravishing side; after much thought I ended up with the blue floral dress, which has always saved me in situations like these?

I love the smell of a baked cake, it always make me feel I have not wasted my talent of baking. Well, someday, I promise myself I will have a bakery shop of my own. Driving down the lane, these thoughts keep me occupied, making me reach the destination much faster than I expected. With a fake smile & an air of arrogance, I prepare myself to enter the new villa of my boss.

People do seem happy & relaxed, after all who would not like a break on a Sunday afternoon & treat themselves with such amount of lavish food. My boss always outdoes himself in parties like these. After all he is a perfectionist, wealthy, high society guy. I wish I could marry a wealthy, loving man like him. I do love my boss & his family, it is just his being hyper about things puts me off sometimes. Otherwise, sometimes he does seem to be the perfect family type guy.

"Hey boss, congratulations for your new home" hugging me in a tight & warm embrace, I know he is very happy at the moment. "Thank you pumpkin, you are late &you know it irritates me" laughing it off, I gave me him a look, saying you know me right. He just ignored me & whispered " I have someone who is a fan of your cake & just the right guy for you to hang out with in this boring party" I was embarrassed, though I know my boss was a very observant man, but it never occurred to me he noticed that I don't really enjoy these parties. I mean I kept my façade on till the end of it.

As we neared this tall, handsome man, suddenly I went all nervous & edgy, well that is the problem with me. As soon as I am introduced to a guy, it just makes me all uncomfortable & shy. My boss introduced him to me "Hi Nihal, she is Naina, the awesome baker I was talking about." As I looked up, I am lost in his blue clear warm eyes. How can a guy have such smouldering & attractive eyes? He brought his hand forward & like a school girl I was just all confused & bewildered. My boss gave me a look, suddenly I realised I need to shake my hand & I did it awkwardly. Nihal who is observing me very keenly, with a hint of smile shake hands firmly. "So, is baking your passion or just something you are good at" I gather myself up & with that gathered confidence "It's my passion and it was a love". He gave me a weird smile and offered a drink.

What is wrong with me, why am being so flirty with him. That isn't me but since I have done, I think I should continue with my newfound talent. Lost in my thoughts, I missed that he was asking me something, "I am sorry, what?" "I was just curious to know, how baking can be a love at first sight" I was at loss of words, I can see he is observing me again & waiting what will be my response. I can also see the smug & naughty look on his face & I instantly know I cannot give him the pleasure of me being caught off guard. So I told him random things which came first in my mind "Actually I use to watch my grandmother cook and the smile she had while cooking made me fall in love with the whole process" seeing him loose his smile, I purposely added "Where you expecting a different answer?" "No, why you asked so?" "Just the look on your face, it seems my answer disappointed you." Laughing loudly he said "no Miss Naina, your presence of mind intrigues me" with that he turned & met someone he knew.

Leaving me to think what did he mean? I politely, excused myself from his company, it was somewhat over powering. Though I loved the perfume he is wearing, his eyes are a different thing altogether. I can just keep looking at them for hours. Turning around I looked for my boss, I wanted to excuse myself from this party as I had other plans with my friends too. As I was saying my goodbyes to my boss and his beautiful wife, Nihal whispered from behind in my ears "Why are you leaving so early?" I was baffled with such closeness. I tilted my head, with a nervous laugh "Have some other plans with my friends". He looked disappointed but then he offered to drop to my destination, "Sorry, I have my car". Something told me, he wanted to spend more time with me & that pleased me but my plan with Riya has been pending for a long time I cannot cancel it for a guy I just met. Giving the briefest smile possible, I said my good byes & left from the party feeling all flustered & excited.

I looked back & I knew his gaze was fixed on me, they were so intense that for once I just felt like cancelling the plan & walk back into the party but I controlled, took heavy steps to my car, sat & drove.

I just could not shake him off from my mind the whole time.

CHAPTER 3

As always, I was late to meet Riya but she being a sweetheart she never makes an issue out of it. In consolation I bought her favourite flowers & chocolates, she knows that I do realise my mistakes. Meeting Riya is always refreshing; she is the most cheerful person I have met in my life. I so want to tell her about my meeting with Nihal but today we are here to sort out Riya's issue. Seeing her all dull & sad makes me nervous about her. "So what's the issue? What is so important & urgent." The beautiful part of our friendship is we never beat around the bush. Riya looks up at me all teary eyed "I think I have to break up with him".

I am all confused, "You have a boyfriend?", Secrets between friends kills it all & Riya knows I hate secrets but then I have to act more mature in this case because today is all about her. "Yeah, I have been dating this guy since 6 months but I never thought I would get so emotionally attached with him".

"Okay, so why are you breaking up with him".

"Well he can't take a stand for me in front of his family & I can't continue with him anymore". I am quiet understanding but then what should I tell her. I was not even informed about this relationship & I have no idea how this guy is? I am looking at her, I have never seen Riya so distraught & broken, and she has always come across as the strongest person to me.

I hug her & tell her things will be okay. In my mind a thought crosses, does this thing get any better from here? I have been through heartaches & they were bad but I never lost hope in love. I think it sweeps up in your life when it has to & your whole life becomes all scattered yet beautiful in its own way. Riya gathers herself & within a fraction of a second she is back to her bubbly self "So what's going on in your life". She always leaves me astonished "Well I met a guy". From there the conversation became light & fun.

"So did you take his phone number?" it was then I realised, we never exchanged numbers or anything personal. It was normal chat but then why I felt so drawn towards him. I kept this thought to myself because Riya being the logical one will give another of her lectures, on how emotional & over imaginative I become about such situations. Very casually I lie to her "it was too soon & I was busy with my boss seeing arrangements" I think she bought it.

We then discussed about our recent shopping adventures & times we have spent together. Sipping our latte's we laughed together, had heart-warming chats, cribbed about our lives & finally we decided to meet again soon.

From there I went home & was all tired that I fell into a peaceful sleep.

CHAPTER 4

People would hate Monday mornings but I think I love them. It means I am back on my daily schedule of jogging in the morning & then ready for my office. I love everything about my job, the big credits goes to my boss for making it so welcoming & interesting. It's been only six months but I enjoy everything about it. My job profile is of an event co-ordinator. Mostly I supervise & do follow up rounds with the banquet managers, still the role I play & the trust my boss shows in me is worthwhile. In addition, it pays me quite well that I can take care of my daily needs, rent & then save some for the future too. Overall profession I feel very happy & satisfied.

Today, for some reason my boss is late, which happens rarely, taking this as an opportunity, I go for a walk near the beach. Another beautiful thing about my office is it is located next to the sea shore. Whenever we are stressed out from the work, all our employees go for a walk near the Samaui beach. It has an instant calming effect on the nerves. Sitting near the sea side, watching waves after waves, I lose myself in time, somewhere from the far distance I can hear a voice calling me but I just cannot seem to move, it was a breath-taking view from here.

As the voice neared me, I realised it's been an hour I have been sitting in this tranquil state, the voice yelled "we have been looking for you, all over, boss is waiting for you, hurry up." I wake up from my dazed state & run behind her, sometimes I am unable to understand what comes over me but right now I have to rush. One thing is for sure, I cannot take my boss for granted if he acts as my friend then he can act bossy too. As I enter the office, my boss fuming with anger gave me a look & I knew I was in thick soup. "Where the hell were you? Didn't know you had to go & meet Mr. Mehta for her daughter's wedding arrangements?" I knew "I thought we were supposed to go together, sir". "No, we were not.

Now stop arguing take these design & leave immediately, he is waiting for you at the Vinear Hotel's Lobby". Instantly I collect the designs & prepare myself to go when my boss gives me a warning which is rare "Naina, I want this deal to be closed today itself. No more, excuses. I hope I have made myself clear" & I knew today is not the morning I was expecting it to be.

As I drove to the hotel, in my mind I kept going over the designs, it was a do or die situation for me. I entered the hotel's lobby with confident & ease, all in my mind I kept thinking today I have to close off this deal. Something inside told me it's not going to be easy to persuade Mr. Mehta. I saw him sitting with his daughter & some relatives. "Hello, Mr. Mehta, I am Naina from Events Paradise, sorry my boss couldn't make it but I have all the designs for the wedding ready, if you may please". "Yeah right, Richard called & told me some family emergency came, so he is sending his second best. I hope you stand up to the expectations of your boss, though you look very young to handle meetings like these". This is what I hate about these meetings, Mr. Mehta is one of the leading industrialists in Mumbai, but then he does not have any right to be rude to me. I think this comes along with my job package. So very politely with a smile "you are right Mr. Mehta, I am too young for this job but my designs are quite unique and as per your taste. So let's not form an opinion beforehand". I knew I have irritated him but then I could not stop myself from answering back, though in my heart I was praying for some miracle to happen.

After showing him all the designs & convincing him of the changes, he finally agreed to give the contract to our company, I was escalated but then Mr. Mehta said "I am only giving you this contract as I have trust in Richard otherwise your designs were not that great. I think you should work more on the intricate details of the designs." Since he was our client & the deals closed, I kept my mouth shut, smiled & left the Hotel with a triumphant feeling.

Sometimes it is okay to let the client think he won, because more than his ego, the money is more important he is going to pay us for our services.

As I enter the office, my fun loving, happy go lucky boss was back. Richard was proud of me, sometimes I imagine Richard as my dad, who is proud of my achievements. Since, he was in such a good mood, he asked me to handle this project solely. It was great opportunity yet it came with its downside. It was one thing to close the deal with Mr. Mehta but working with him day & night was not on my priority list. I tried my best to explain Richard "I am too young for this whole venture; I think Hemant has an expertise in handling weddings like these".

"No way, I have made my decision; you are going to handle this wedding. Mr. Mehta was so impressed the way you handled his queries & responded".

I was surprised "he was, because I was under the impression, we got the deal because of you".

"Oh C'mon, Naina you always have underestimated yourself, I always knew you can out do others" I smiled as I knew my boss cannot be deterred from this & somewhere I again had this uneasy feeling that my month is going to be very eventful from now on.

Before leaving Richard told me "tomorrow you would be shifting to Mr. Mehta's farm house & would supervise from there, it would save the time". I knew this was going to be eventful did not expect it to start so soon.

CHAPTER 5

Remember I said I love weekdays but now I am regretting it. I have to prepare and leave for Mr. Mehta's farmhouse in an hour. I have to pack & clean my house, inform my tenant, I am already feeling home sick. After an hour, finishing my to do list, I call for a cab & get ready for the first big sow assignment of my life. I have always waited for this opportunity, only I thought my boss would be helping me in it, not leaving me alone. During the drive I tried to keep myself all excited and positive about the opportunity but I kept on failing. The only saviour of my life, I called my mom & explained the whole situation.

"Naina, you over think things sometimes too much. Stop judging people, it can be a turning point of your life". My mom is the most positive soul on this earth she can find positivity in the worst possible situations & can make you feel better about it. Sometimes I think, only if I had two percent of her positivity, I would have been much better as a person in my life. "Okay mom, you are right, maybe I am overthinking it". "Of course you are, now work hard & make me proud. Do not make me regret the decision of sending you so far alone, just to crib about the situations in your life. Be smooth & feel the love in whatever you are doing. Do meditate; it will bring the calmness in you". Yeah, solution to all the problems, Meditate; this time for a change I agree with mom, I am being very judgemental about the situation & people. "Thank you mom, you just saved me on this. I think now I am up for the job. Let's kill it, of course with a smile". "That's like my daughter love and take care".

Talk like these with mom always make me feel blessed & grateful for having her around. Here, as I enter the farm house, Oh-My-God, it's huge and lavish. It is indeed the best event opportunity I could ever get, mentally; I thank my boss & prepare myself for this opportunity.

Are all the rooms this spacious or am I been given the most spacious one? As I look around, I am pleased with the whole ambience & decorative pieces around the room. Mr. Mehta is one classy man, I decided, maybe I was wrong about him. I now understand why he was so uncertain about some designs specifications. I takeout the designs & start making some modifications, as I feel that would be appropriate according to the place. After the changes, I decided to take a tour of the place before the whole family arrives. However, my work starts after two days, but I have to arrange things beforehand and I don't want to delay the arrangements. With being particular, Mr. Mehta is also punctual. He had handed over me the timings of each event and has given me deadlines, by which all arrangements should be ready.

As I was making the tour, I had this feeling someone was watching me, but when I turned I could not see anyone. This was strange, I kept going from one room to another, analysing, deciding what & how we can change the décor & design the room according to the functions. As I was checking the last room, I heard a click, instantly I looked back but there was no one around. Scared I made my way out of the room & there I saw those blues eyes looking directly at me from behind the door. I was shocked, elated & flustered, all at the same time. Was that even remotely possible? Then putting on my best smile, I looked up "Hi, nihal, good to see you again". Again, that smug smile & intense gaze, it makes me so nervous but kept up the façade "Hi, Naina, are you a friend of Neha?" I was confused, "Neha, who?" "Neha, the bride, who is getting married" "oohhh" is all that I can say. In my whole cribbing about the situation, I forgot to ask about the bride and the groom names and their details. I made a note that I need to meet them, as they play vital role in deciding the colour combinations.

"Oohh! Is that all are you going to give me" I realised I have not given him an answer, God he is so over powering "No, I am the event co-ordinator for the wedding". Then with a huge smile, which was beautifully spread across his perfect lips "and you are not aware of the name of bride or the groom". Wow, he found something to pull my leg about. Then suddenly a thought came, is he the groom & my heart start beating faster than ever. I asked "Are you the groom". With that smile he answered "Do you want me to be?" At that moment I decided, I am never going to get a straight answer from him ever. "Well, it's your life your choice" I said as matter of fact. On that he gave a full hearty laugh "No, I am the friend of groom" & kept smiling, observing me.

Since I had nothing to say more, so I excused myself but he interrupted "today too, you have a friend to attend to", for a moment I lost him & then it registered he is referring to our last meeting & that brought an instant smile on my face so he remembers me well enough, "No, just doing my job". With a nod, he turned towards the room & I thought the conversation is over but then he whispered "I love the way you smile, it just takes away years from you" & he disappeared. For I don't know how long I just kept standing there, looking into the space, it was the best compliment I have received.

Guys like him are a danger bell, that's what Riya would tell me & warn about but this pulls me towards him. I mean I have dated guys off & on but he was different & I knew I had to keep distance from with. On that note, I completed my rest of the round, made notes & mailed them to Mr. Mehta. The evening dinner was served in my room, I went for a walk, hoping to see him again but there were no signs of him. Maybe he just came to check on the rooms & left. Feeling exhausted from the drive & work, I decided to retire to my room as tomorrow the whole Mehta & Chopra families would arrive and early morning, tomorrow I have to start with my decorations arrangement too.

CHAPTER 6

I woke up to loud noises outside my door. It took me a minute to realise it was not my apartment. Both the families had arrived & I was running late, so I hurriedly ran to the bathroom to get ready. As I stepped out of the room, outside was a mess with suitcases, travel bags, suddenly the lobby did not look like the same; that I had come to yesterday. That is the effect of Punjabi families they can just change the whole ambience of the room within minutes.

After excusing myself from dozens of aunties I finally found Mr. Mehta who was standing next to Nihal. It's my first assignment, with toughest client & on top of that Nihal's over powering presonality, I knew I am doomed. Mentally, I prayed to god to infuse some of my mom's positivity in me for the whole situation. As I reached Mr. Mehta, Nihal fixed his eyes on me I got nervous & worked up again. With a straight face I enquired if he liked the changes Mr. Mehta "Well I liked few changes but I would still prefer you to discuss with my daughter before ordering the flowers" "Okay, where can I find her. As it is I want to meet bride & the groom for their opinions too." satisfied with my response Mr. Mehta asked Nihal to take me to the bride & the groom. In my mind, I thought, cannot god be a little kind to me at times.

"Pleasure is all mine" I gave him a clipped smile & followed him through. "So baking is your passion, rather love at first sight (smiling again) & by profession you are an event co-ordinator. Are there any more surprises stored in?"

"Yes, as a person I don't like being stared at or inquired about so much". I was so irritated with the whole situation, that before I could stop myself, I said it aloud. Strangely, he kept quiet after that till we located the bride & the groom. On the way I side-glanced him two three times, all I could see was a straight face without any emotion. I do not know what he thought about me at that moment, but I cared & that fact irritated me even more.

Sitting in front of the bride & the groom, I felt they were like a picture perfect couple. So much in love, I prayed to God, when I would find one, then diverting my mind to work. I asked them questions, about how they met, who proposed, what are their favourite colours, showed them designs & asked for their opinions. They were the easiest and the most understanding couple I have come across. These were the first ones appreciate my work earnestly, after which I became even more positive & motivated about the whole event. Their energy & love in the whole room was infectious. I decided then, they were that perfect couple, people looked up in magazines.

Satisfied, I got up to leave; Nihal blocked my way & asked me to come for a walk with him. This guy can easily baffle you up, "Well I did not mean to irritate you, all I wanted was to strike a conversation". At that moment I felt embarrassed for my weird behaviour, "I did not mean to be rude", is all I could say. Then with a smile, "All's clear between us. Tell me what's your story?". This guy was impossible. Had I not made myself clear, I am not interested. I told him politely "I am here for a job assignment & not on wedding trip. So if you don't mind can I continue with my job please?" to this he laughed so hard, I couldn't understand. Then suddenly very seriously, he told me "I like it when you mask your feelings behind this serious face. By the way, your eyes say it all & sometimes your face gives it away. I think you should know". Since I did not know how to respond to this, I turned around & left for the job, I was paid for.

Rest of the afternoon went very smoothly, with decoration team doing their best; all the supplies came in time. Flowers were fresh & beautiful. Even the gold rings ordered at the last moment, came in time too. Days like this in my life are rare. I spared myself a smile & a walk around the place. I was tired standing there, guiding people & making everything look perfect. I realised I missed my lunch & was starving. Since I did not know whether I should go to kitchen or table counters, I decided I could live with the pack of biscuit in my handbag.

A cup of coffee, after such a tiring day is like heaven to me; While I was having my coffee my mind again drifted to Nihal our last conversation. Am I so predictable or does he notice me a lot? For the first time in my life I was at a loss of words & clueless about a guy. A part of me told me, he was just having fun at his friend's wedding but another part argued what if he is genuinely interested! I have just known him for three days. Then came a voice from behind "Were you thinking about me because I saw you smiling", caught red handed I blushed but did not spoke a word.

Throwing his hands up & smiling "I was just pulling your leg. If you don't mind can I join you for a cup of coffee".

"Mine is almost finished, you can enjoy yours alone".

"C'mon Naina throw me some slack, a coffee with me wouldn't cost your job but would give a good company to enjoy". Reluctantly I agreed, as I wanted to spend time with him.

"You still have not answered my question"

"Which question?"

"Except baking & event co-ordinator, what else you do?"

"I go home & sleep". I smiled then continued "Well, my job takes most of my day, I hardly get time to pursue anything else".

"Hmmm. But if you would have time, what would you like to do?"

"Why are you so much interested in knowing about me?"

"Well, I am just striking a conversation, but I don't know why you end up taking it so personally". Then I realised he is right, it is just a conversation, why do I become so edgy & conscious around him. What is wrong with me? I needed to figure it out soon.

"Sorry, I think the work takes its toll over me. I would love to learn Jazz, if ever given a chance."

"Okay. Baker, event co-ordinator & a dancer too; You are quite a package, Naina". To this, I looked up & tried to find if he is making fun of me but no, he was serious. The admiration showed on his face. I just could not take my eyes off his face. Then on cue, he looked up directly into my eyes "Are you engaged?"

"No, I am single", I thought why am I giving him so much information but his gaze was so intense I couldn't stop myself from answering.

"Good". After a long pause, very slowly he added "For me". He got up, came close to me, smiled and whispered, "I am single too" with that, he left.

Perplexed as I was, his closeness left goose bumps all over my body. After a minute or so, it hit me hard; he cannot just come by & walk off a conversation whenever he wants. I promise, next time I will make sure, I clear this thing between us. Angrily, I got up from the lawn, went to see the decorations & stopped for the day. I was so pissed with him & myself, I decided to skip the dinner.

The whole night went tossing & turning in anger.

CHAPTER 7

I could not sleep the whole night. The effect, Nihal's closeness had left on me was unforgettable. There was a constant fight between my head & heart. I knew I was attracted to him but the way I feel around him, all edgy & nervous, is something unexplainable. My head shout aloud, I need to keep my distance from him. After much thought I decided, I do not want to get involved with him in any way possible. To sort my head, I got up at 5 am & went for jogging. I knew nobody would disturb me at this hour in the farmhouse.

The jog helped; well it has always helped me in sorting things out in my head. The exhilaration & euphoria I get from jogging have a calming effect on my mind. The farmhouse is a beautiful place to jog around, since everyone was into deep slumber; I took advantage of the situation & jogged for another 15 minutes. Only I wish I had not, would have walked right in to my room but then I did not know.

As I was taking my last round I again had this feeling someone was watching me, turned my head & there was Nihal calm as ever with a brooding gaze. I stopped in my tracks, exhausted from running, for once I did not want to think anything just wanted to enjoy this moment looking at his perfect physique. He was wearing boxers & a tee, he was looking damn right sexy. He had this lazy air about him, his eyes never left mine, the whole time it felt as if he was gauging me. I on other hand was mesmerised by the way he looked. Secretly I was drawn to him; there were butterflies in my stomach & heartbeat accelerated to a rate where I think I would need an oxygen mass to breath. I always thought, do things like these happen to people or are these just some lines written in a novel or felt in movies only? But here I was feeling the emotions that too with intensity I have never felt before for any of the guys I have met so far.

I had a feeling, he was waiting for me to approach him but that's something never going to happen, at least not now here where I have a job to do. I took a deep breath in & continued jogging to my room. I just did not want to take a risk to stop & look back. I could not bear to look at his smug smile, my response towards him, have shown him my vulnerability & it was clear by my gaze and expressions that I am attracted to him. I cannot just let him have that satisfaction of 'I know'. I have too much pride to let any guy ever know how much he affects me. Taking a hot shower bath, relaxing the tense muscles, I got ready for the day. My agenda for today is "IGNORE NIHAL AT ANY COST".

Finally, after an hour I started listening to hustle & bustle in the farmhouse. It made me so happy, somehow here people around me made me safe. Tonight was a small function "Dholki Night", which only the families were to attend. I planned a light decoration with hint of orchids, as the bride is in love with orchids. Everything was pastel coloured matching with the bride's outfit. I was quite satisfied with the way the decoration of the whole place was coming out like. With small goof ups which comes with the package otherwise everything came out really well. It had to, Mr. Mehta was still not very confident about my handling event alone. Well, he had called my boss at least 20 times, expressing his doubts about my work. My boss being a sweetheart, he in his own way had silenced the doubts of Mr. Mehta. I seriously, do not know how my boss handles clients like him; I still have to learn tactics. I was so thankful to my boss for backing me up every time I needed.

Being so busy with the arrangements, I dint realise it was 4pm already. I decided to call Mr. Mehta, so that he can give his suggestions if he needed some changes which I was very sure he would suggest. Mr. Mehta inspected the whole place as if a detective finding some fault in the crime scene, it was hard for me to control my laughter. I knew I have done quite a work above his expectation after all my boss had instructed me, finding any mistake was little difficult. I could see Mr. Mehta smiling though he pointed out some mistakes but I was escalated with a fact he had a smile on his face. It felt like, I have passed my boards examination with 90%, which was quite satisfactory.

I love days like these, when the days are filled with hard work & night with rest. Well, I am a workaholic by nature but I do need my weekend breaks with occasional adventurous trips, if I may add so. I called my boss, I was very happy with my first success; I wanted to celebrate it with my friends & family. As always my boss came as rescuing guard for me, "Why don't you take a break, come this weekend to Mumbai" I was all up for the idea, I needed break & a date, squealing on the phone, I readily accepted the offer. As it is we had almost a week for the next function & I needed some materials from Mumbai to transport. It will make my life & work both easy.

I informed Mr. Mehta about the changes in the plan. Convincing him the materials have to be transported in my supervision only. "Okay, Miss Naina but I hope you will be back before the next function, because it's a huge one & many of our relatives from abroad are going to attend it. I don't want any mistakes happening". Why can't he for once take me as a professional rather than an amateur, with a smile "of course Mr. Mehta, I will be back by Wednesday with all the supplies & my workers will be here getting the stage & other things ready". He nodded & left.

Before I could leave, Nihal blocked my way "You are leaving again?" Since I was in a good mood, I decided to be little flirtatious with him. "Well, I never had decided to stay for long" his smile was back "Well, if I would have asked you to, would you have stayed" he caught me off guard. I did not want to sound rude neither and I want to grab this opportunity. Guys have never been this straight forward to me, they have always been cheesy, the reason I don't have a comeback for this one as usual.

I started blabbering "umm… I need to go, as I need some space & then I need to go celebrate with my friends, I have supplies to pick, I have these designs to discuss with my boss, staying back would be boring" after I finish my incomplete sentences, I look up into his warm eyes & his smile "Have a nice weekend, ahead Naina". With that he was about to leave, when I stopped him & cleared "Mr. Nihal, whatever your surname is, you cannot just come by & start a conversation whenever you want & leave whenever you feel like. That's not the way" I was quite angry & breathless by the time I finished. Since he was tall, he bent a little "I am sorry, I did not realise I was doing that". Taken aback, I was expecting him to throw attitude or his smug smile but he genuinely apologised. I just nod & left.

The whole time, in my room I replayed the conversation we had; I became more confused about him. "urrghhh" I shouted into my pillow. Can't my life be just plain simple sometimes, I hoped. I packed my stuff & was relieved; tomorrow I will be back home.

With this thought, I slept like a baby the whole night.

CHAPTER 8

I love long drives & the drive from farmhouse to Mumbai is a splendid one. In times like this, I can only think of my closest friend Nemish, we have shared so many drives like this. Instantly I called him

"Hi, sweetheart" Nemish was surprised; it's been six months since we spoke.

"Hi babes, how have you been?"

"Are you free tonight, let's go out for a dinner".

"Yea, okay. Meet @7 then."

"Great, love yea".

I am already excited for tonight's dinner. It's been ages & he is the only one I can speak my heart out with. Finally, after 3 hours, I am home. Exhausted to the core but then excited to meet Nemish. I took the dress he gave me on my birthday, he loves to see me all dolled up & somewhere I love to get dressed for him. With Nemish life seemed beautiful, almost picturesque.

Nemish was awed by the way I look, he appreciated beauty, and he is the most expressive guy I have known. He himself looked quite dashing in those rugged jeans & a simple tee. He can pull off anything that is the thing, I admire about him very much. Table was pre-booked, it was our favourite place with light music in background, gave us time to talk our heart out. He updated me about his work, the new girl in his life & the trips he has been having with her. I was happy for him, it felt nice in such a young age he have achieved so much & had someone to share with. Just sitting in his company, listening to his achievements made me feel at home, he had that aura around him, you instantly feel at home.

We ordered our favourite pasta & lasagne; it's the best on the menu here. I told him about my new assignment and how its been coming out. Then I told him about Nihal, how I feel and how much he affects me? All the while I was talking; he had this irresistible smile on his face, which made me uncomfortable about the whole situation.

"What, why are you smiling like an idiot"

"You really want to know or you want me to listen to whatever you saying?" it made me all the more confuse

 "Okay, I am listening"

With a sigh he continued "Naina, you have fallen for this guy & you are fighting it hard not to. I would suggest you just go with the flow. Not every time you have to find logic in every situation." It made sense, but I was sure I was attracted to him & not in love.

I kept quiet after that because Nemish is the only person who will not judge me or pass on an opinion like this. Well our dinners always ended with a long walk near the sea. With a clear sky & light breeze, for a moment I forgot everything & just enjoyed being here. Lying down on sand, looking up at stars, with smile on our faces, we could have spent the whole night like this. Then my phone buzzed & boss on line.

"Hello, boss what happened?"

"Naina, tomorrow morning we have meeting with new clients & I want you to head it as Shyla is not well."

 "What time should I be there?"

"Be there by 8:30 & call Shyla, ask her to brief you with the designs".

"Yes, boss will do".

Sometimes work has its own way of spoiling moments like these. I looked at Nemish & he knew it's time to leave me home. On the way I called Shyla, she briefed me up with the designs & was thankful for the last moment help. Saying goodbye to Nemish was always difficult. May be because I knew it would be long wait when I meet him again or maybe he is the one with whom life seems worth living around. There were always mixed feelings, so I hugged him long enough before the good byes came.

Smiling I thanked the universe for the beautiful evening today, before I opened my laptop to study the designs for the new client tomorrow.

Again I was late, I saw the clock it was 7:30 already, I ran to get dressed, I don't even remember when I dozed off in between studying the designs, I am not fully prepared for the meeting too. Choosing clothes for meetings like this have always been a difficult task; mentally I made a note to join Zumba classes as I have to reduce the extra fat. I decided to wear something ethnic as it made me look more presentable. In a rush I reached office, I was 10 minutes late; hurriedly I entered the cabin excusing myself for being late. All the three men sitting in front were extremely handsome & polished. Instantly, I regretted my choice of clothes today.

Richard introduced me to the clients, unfortunately, all three were married, I smiled inside my head when they checked me out with the corner of their eyes. After briefing men up with the idea, I started showing them the designs, which Shyla had made for their upcoming office. Well the meeting went for almost two hours, with a quite amount of changes in the designs & price negotiations. For the most part of the meeting, I observed how convincing my boss could be once he set his mind on.

After lunch, I went to Richard to discuss with Mr. Mehta's design for the next function. To my astonishment the whole setting's changed,

I was aghast to know that, I argued "boss, how I will be able to incorporate so many changes, so early?"

"Naina, you have the contacts of every supplier, use them & arrange things, you have only 2 hours left, also you have to rush back to farm house to instruct these changes", saying this my boss left with a broad smile. I looked at the designs for few minutes more & then I was on phone the whole after noon.

By 7pm I had arranged all the supplies needed for the event, for the whole time I was shouting, begging, howling on the phone. It's not an easy thing to arrange things on such short notice. I owed favour to almost 10 people for coming to my aid. I was exhausted to the core; I slept through the entire drive to the farmhouse.

Tomorrow I knew it's going to be very hectic. First things first I need to call meeting of all the workers to inform the changes in the design.

Till 2 am, I was up with the decorators, showing them the supplies & the changes that were to be made. Hopefully they understood with a reluctant yes. When you are an event coordinator, the luxury of sleep is something you do not get that easily. We were all up by 5, with coffee's & fake enthusiasm we started working for the event. Early mornings are boon to us, with no hustle bustle around; we can work peacefully & quickly.

At 10am, I called in for a break, as everyone was tired. After an hour break, with my tummy filled with parantha's I was all set to work. I knew the outside decoration will be handled by my assistant, so I totally engrossed myself with the hall decorations. According to the theme, we had decided to decorate the hall with bangles, kalira's & drapes of chunni's (everything included in an

Indian bride's get up). I loved this part of the wedding events, there are very close to my heart.

I knew there was constant smile on my face, it always does happen when I involve myself with the decorating team. While I was finding & re-arranging the bangles, I saw Nihal walking towards me. My heart did some dance of it's own, finally he found me. I had this huge smile plastered on my lips

"Hi Nihal, how have you been?"

"Good. I thought you left the job."

Still smiling widely I replied "No, just stuck in some meetings. So, how are the groom & everyone." In my mind, I wanted to ask did you miss me but then that's all I came up with.

"All messed up, I think" and we both laughed. "If you don't mind, can I help you with this."

"Sure, actually I need hands to sort out this". I explained him how it should be done.

For the first time with Nihal, I had a good conversation; I came to know he is into garment industry & keeps travelling between Canada & Mumbai. He loves travelling & has travelled half of the globe. He is a foodie & I was shocked to know he has tasted quite a few things that I had baked for my boss. He is related to my boss wife, so his trips to their home are quite frequent. He is a movie buff. All the while I kept asking him questions & he kept answering patiently.

I realised I like his voice & the way he thinks first before answering any question. I was looking at his face, his eyes, the crease near his nose, I think he noticed, he looked up & caught me staring at him. With a raised brow he looked at me & then ever so slowly winked.

Raising his hands he announced, "I am done, boss"

I realised he sorted out all the stuff while I was staring at him. I smiled sheepishly & said "Thank you".

"Pleasure all mine." After a pause, he asked "Would you like to take a walk in the evening".

I looked around the hall; there still a lot of work to be done, though my heart kept telling me to say yes, sensing my hesitation he added "I don't sleep early". To this I smiled, agreed for the walk at 11pm.

"Deal, it is" he shook hands & with a bow he left, I couldn't stop myself from laughing hard. It was funny the way he bowed. With this thought & a smile I went back to work. I was undoubtedly in a very good mood, was sweet to my workers, giggling with them, singing songs, every one noticed the change in my mood. I dint even shout when one of the girls mishandled few of the supplies. I think everyone loved me like this. I did too.

CHAPTER 9

I was waiting for clock to strike 11. Even with so much work, my eyes inevitably did not forget to check time. It felt as though the time has almost stopped and has forgotten to move forward. As soon as it was 10:30, I ran to my room, to take a look on myself. I wanted to look good & I did manage to do so.

I left for the place we decided to meet; it was backside of the farmhouse, a beautiful park with sculptures, flowers all around & in the middle, there was a big bench. The whole place was magical & colourful. As I was taking in the beauty of the place, I saw Nihal in his jeans & tee he looked breathtakingly handsome. For a moment, I wished I could stop the clock right there. He gave me one of his best smiles and asked me to accompany him to the bench in the middle.

Quietly I followed him, we sat there awkwardly, and silently both of us lost in our own thoughts. I looked at him sideways, I could see him smiling, I waited for him to start the conversation but looking at his face it felt he is quite happy being here sitting quietly like this.

Impatient as I am, I asked, "So what is making you give such a broad smile?"

His intense looks were back, they make me feel so uncomfortable "Nothing, it's the whole atmosphere actually, I like it here".

"Hmmm", I was clueless now, I decided to calm my nerves but then his next question made me more conscious.

"So have you been in a relationship?" Mostly I am very open about my relationships but somehow here I just did not want to give away the details.

Very cautiously, slowly I told him, "I have been out on a number of dates but there have been two serious relationships."

He nodded, "So how did you meet Richard?"

"Well, a friend of mine introduced me to him, I told him I am in need of a job & he offered me a trainee position first, later I think I was capable enough to be his employee & a part of his family too". I added with a warmth & smile remembering the time I got introduced to my boss, Richard.

"Why?"

"Just like that, Richard & his family speak very highly of you & they are so fond of you & your cakes".

I was thinking if, Richard has spoken about me to Nihal, why and what did he tell him. I need to speak to him first thing in the morning. Lost in my thoughts, I did not notice, that Nihal was observing me. Settling my thoughts when I looked at him, he was now sitting closer to me. I could not take my eyes off his lips, they were so kissable, controlling myself I looked up in his eyes & I saw them changing into darker shade of blue. I did not know whether I should move forward or stay still. Then ever so slowly he moved in closer & touched my lips, my whole body went on fire. He kept pressing feather light kisses on my mouth taking his own time, sliding his tongue on my lower lip, asking permission to deepen the kiss. I opened my mouth letting him in, his tongue touched mine & I lost all control. I held on to his tee, pulling him closer; desire took over me with a pace I never knew existed in me before. Before this, I always had control over myself, but the way he was kissing me, exploring my mouth, something inside me opened up. Later I thought how tender yet passionate the kiss was. Not once he forced himself upon, he definitely knew how to coax a reaction out of women.

As our lips parted, he cupped my cheeks & looked directly into my eyes. I was breathless, shy but the gentleness I saw in his eyes, held mine for a little longer. I looked away, feeling embarrassed. He moved a little closer & said, "it was quite intense for you, wasn't it?"

Suddenly, my logical mind was back & I asked "What was this kiss for Nihal, what do you want from me?" I wanted to know what was going in his mind.

With turmoil going on in my mind, his voice sounded quite calm "I like you Naina, but it is just this physical attraction or what I am not sure. I don't want to play with you and your feelings so I am being blunt."

One part of my mind shouted to leave him and run never look back but the illogical one argued to at least he is being truthful. What did I want? Another fling, which I know I cannot handle, as I get emotionally attached to the person & this one has already started affecting me. After much fight within me, I decided, I do not want any other fling. I wanted a man to stick by me forever & however I am.

With a firm face, I looked at Nihal, who was observing me the whole time "I can't Nihal. I do not want any other fling in my life. I want a commitment & may be after sometime marriage but not a fling".

His face was expressionless "I can't commit anything Naina, it's too soon."

"Sorry, I can't play around anymore, if your idea is just having fun, I don't want to play that part."

Saying this I got up & left, there were tears in my eyes, his casual response towards me had hit me hard. Harder than I thought, I felt betrayed, I realised I cared & I hated myself for that.

I directly went to my room and for almost an hour, I cried. I cried like a baby, exactly the same way I cried when Dhruv betrayed me.

CHAPTER 10

Dhruv was the dream changed into reality. We were introduced through a friend over a slice of pizza. He was a charmer, a dancer, influential & prejudiced. Our first meeting ended in a fight over some religious issues. After that we met again on my best friend's birthday, slowly he became the part of the group. I still remember, his first message, when he was concerned about my friend's health & he wanted to know how I am doing. I found it strange, but then I knew he was close to my best friend, so gave him a benefit of doubt.

Then it started with a chain of messages, to phone calls, all was very casual until one day when he confessed his love for me. I was shaken so out rightly said no. It took him three months to convince me about the relationship. It was the most magical time of my life. I used to wake up with a bunch of roses lying at my doorstep. Sometimes I used to get love letters with declarations of love & passion. He left no stone unturned in making me believe his love for me was true. Finally, I gave in & a beautiful chapter of my life started.

For a year, everything was like a fairy tale then suddenly it went topsy-turvy. He started keeping too much busy with his clients; he used to get irritated with late night calls. He started avoiding my calls and messages. Initially it was for few days & then it went on for a month. Being an emotional fool, I used to wait for his call or message day in & day out. Fights on petty reasons started happening, suddenly my weight became an issue for physical intimacy. He took away my self-confidence, my zeal in life & most importantly my smile.

It happened so quickly, I could not fathom to what went wrong between us. We decided to give our relation one last chance and met for a coffee. Everything went smooth, he realised his mistakes, even I apologised for being so uncompromising at times. In my heart I thought our relationship could work out. It was then when he left his mobile on the table & went to the restroom, it beeped & without thinking much, I picked up.

It was a message "I love you but we can't be together forever".

My whole world came sprawling to an end. I read the whole chat & it shocked me to know he had proposed to this girl last year. Everything made sense, irritation for late night calls, avoiding me for months, my weight issues, my being too emotional & clingy. When he came back, with a teary eyed I asked him why?

He shouted, "how dare you see my messages?"

I kept quiet & looked at him, how could I trust someone again. How could I be so wrong about a person? Where did I go wrong? I just could not bring myself to terms with the fact of him cheating on me. I left him standing there fuming in anger.

I went into deep depression. Months went by and I still could not digest the fact, he cheated on me. In my heart, I still hope he would call & clear out the mess but it never came. Thankfully, after six months with a heavy heart I wrote an email to Nemish. He came as a wave of fresh air in my life. He stayed by my side, taught me to love myself again, taught me to laugh and live life king size. Within a month time's I started opening up to life again. He took a decision, took me to Mumbai and made me meet Richard. Life from there has been magical throughout and until I met Nihal.

I knew my face would be puffy, since I spent the whole night crying. Nihal noticed it but he never approached me. I liked that he kept his distance as I was fuming with anger from inside. All I wanted was to finish the event and run back to my friends and my little apartment. I hate complicating things and the last thing I wanted in my life, was a complicated relationship. One thing I learnt from my dad at early stages of my job was to keep personal and professional lives separate. However, difficult it may seem but that was the only life-line I had to stick to.

With a smile I passed my days in the farm house keeping busy in the event & avoiding Nihal as much as I could. We came in contact two or three times, I knew he wanted to talk but I always made some excuse & left the place. In my heart I was afraid of falling for him. On top of that everything around me was falling apart, for the event the decoration pieces fell short, and few of my workers had food poisoning. My boss & Mr. Mehta were becoming impatient with delays in the decoration. Inside I felt like crying, outside I wore a mask of indifference, tried my best to sort out the mess.

By evening things were better & close to finishing off. While I was working with the lighting people, Mr. Mehta had another issue in hand to resolve, "Ms. Naina, though hiring your company meant I should be free from hassles in the wedding, but it seems like I cannot enjoy even a bit of it"

I was embarrassed "I am sorry Mr. Mehta".

"Can you please sort out the mandap arrangements with Pandit ji, he needs a few things."

I went directly to Pandit ji, he gave me a list of things he needed to be arranged also with the guidelines for seating arrangement guidelines. Luckily, I had kept Mandap arrangements for the last; this saved me time for lightings & stage decorations. I called up my dedicated team members who were looking after the mandap arrangements. Sometimes delegating work makes your life much easier & sorted. The team arrived at around 9pm, after a tea session we all threw ourselves into work. It was a morning wedding with an evening dinner party.

By the time we finished with the whole set it was morning already. I went around the whole place, checked it for over last time. Its been 48 hours since I slept, so I sat near the mandap for a while.

Wedding day is the most beautiful day for the bride & groom. The Pheras, the Var-mala, everything is such an auspicious part of the whole ceremony. I have often dreamt about my big day, the way I would dress, the way the whole setting would be, everything is so vivid and clear in my head. Somewhere, I chose this profession because it helps me live my dream for real. Sitting there imagining myself in this mandap, takes me to my dream world. The mandap setting was exactly the way I wanted on my wedding day. As usual lost in my own world I missed noticing Nihal standing behind me.

"It is a beautiful set, your team has done an amazing work." His remark bought me back to reality.

"Thank you. Couple like Neha & Kunal so much in love, deserves a beautiful memory indeed".

"True. After all the basis of any love story is attraction". He was directly looking in to my eyes.

"Hmmmm." I did not want to argue further. I knew he would not let me go till he has finished talking. I waited for him to continue.

"Naina, all I am asking is to give us time. We have not even gone on a date. Please let's give whatever it's between us, a second chance". I was confused, what it is between us. Keeping my thoughts aside, I gave him my best smile.

"After the wedding here, come with me for a dinner date". Watching my expressions carefully he asked.

"Dinner sounds good. Let me get back to Mumbai, we will plan out something." I purposely took the matters in my hand. I needed time to think & be calm enough to approach him again.

He saved his number in my phone "I hope I will receive a call from you soon". He had doubts & I never cleared them, smiling I walked away from him.

CHAPTER 11

Sitting in the flight, lost in my own thoughts was something rarely I did. I was happy as I was flying back home. Immediately after the event, I took a week's break and took first flight home. I was missing my parents, the comforts of my home. I forced myself to sleep, as it was difficult to stop thinking about Nihal and our first kiss. How many times for the past few days I felt like giving him a call, meet him for a date. I could not bring myself up to it. I knew the date would not be a simple date, I so wanted to kiss him again, be in his arms, feels his lips near my neck, and the thought of it makes me so warm from inside. I have no idea how I will be able to keep my heart safe from him.

Reaching home, seeing my mom almost after seven months feels like heaven. Everything is the same in the house especially my room, it is exactly the way I left it behind. Being with mom, eating my favourite food had made me forget everything. Just being with her makes me feel light from inside, I decided to take advice from mom about Nihal.

"Mom, I wanted to tell you something but I want you to hear it as my friend not as a mother" instantly she replied "Who's the guy?". Surprised I look at her, how does she know what is going on in my mind. Shaking my head visibly I told her the whole story.

"Okay, so when are you planning your next date" Really is she not listening to what all I have said, I emphasised again "Mom I think I can fall for him, so I am avoiding him". My mom looked exasperated with my sentence "Naina just because you think you can fall for him that does not mean you will stop giving it a chance. Before you argue, listen to me. I have no understanding why do you keep underestimating yourself. You are beautiful and intelligent girl. It could be possible that Nihal also likes you, with these dates may be he wants to be sure about him and you never know it could lead to the romance you have always been looking for."

The possibility of Nihal falling for me is too good to be true. I contemplated on mom's words, I know she is right-one wrong relationship, should not be the reason to eliminate love from my life, if that it is so. I need to plan things out, before giving call to Nihal. I had two days in hand to sort things in my mind I really hope, for once, I can just loosen up and live in the moment.

With that thought I got up to refill my tea, enveloped in a warm hug from behind, without looking behind I knew it was my brother Neel. He is not the expressive one, his hugs and smiles are more than enough to let me know he is happy to see me. Ah! How I missed home, I had not realised it until now. In this moment, I know even if things did not work out with Nihal I always have my family to turn to. They will keep me safe, protected, wrapped up in love for all my life.

Soon my holidays were over ended, as I was packing, my bags Neel came to me "Di, I am really proud of you the way you have moulded your life, I know how difficult it is for you and if you ever need me, I am there". I was surprised, by his words, sometimes he really behave as the elder one in us, I just gave him a hug as I was doubtful I could speak with a lump in my throat which was forming now. He held me tighter and whispered "Give life a chance it cannot be bad twice and you were never the one to give up on love" I shifted and saw him smile.

I knew mom had told him everything, as if on cue, my mom decided to enter my room and I gave her a look. Innocently she ignored my look and started lecturing me on health food habits how careless I have become. I decided to let it go, as I knew she wouldn't admit it, then giving her one of her nasty smiles she handed me a poly bag, I opened and found few dresses, lacy lingerie in it. Shocked I looked up at her with a raised eyebrow;

she just shrugged and left the room. Laughing loudly I echoed behind her "Thank you mom, you saved me the trip". Exasperated I look up to the sky and could not thank enough for the amazing family I have. With a heavy heart, I was ready to leave for the job and life waiting for me.

I purposely booked my return for Saturday night, so that I could unpack on Sunday, also I was planning to meet Nihal, provided if he is still interested. It has been more than a week and I have not messaged or called him.

So I texted, "Hi, Naina here, how are you?" and I waited for the reply. I realised I was very nervous and my heart was beating erratically, every second felt like an hour. After ten minutes, he replied.

"Hi, and I thought you would never message". He *"thought"*, he was thinking about me, I was escalated visibly jumping out of joy and then I realised I am at the airport, I sobered up and texted back.

"Sorry, was busy. I was thinking if we can meet up?" I did not feel like explaining him through messages, where was I.

"Sure. Is tonight good for you?" he spoke my mind, which means he is equally excited to meet me. The feeling is exquisite and heady too.

"Perfect. How about 8pm at La Course" it was one of the fine dining places with a lounge and the perfect sea view.

"Nice choice. Meet you at 8". With a smile on my face, I entered the plane and slipped into sweet oblivion.

CHAPTER 12

Nihal

Finally, after much wait, Naina messaged me. I thought I lost her; she would never take that first step. I still remember the first time, when I saw her at Richard's house warming party, she looked beautiful so conscious, she crossed the path I knew she was attracted to me, I wanted to know more about her and I wanted that carefree look in her eyes, which had drawn me towards her. The way she keeps on shifting between being a little flirty and cautious with me on the first day was very refreshing. I was confused about her reaction; I never thought she would avoid me. That is what exactly she did; she even rejected my invitation to drop her house. I could not understand her reactions and kept searching, praying that she would change her mind but nothing. With that one intense look, in which I was sure I saw hesitation and confusion as if she was contemplating the option of staying back but then she stunned me by walking towards her car.

For the coming days, I could not take her out of my mind. I thought once my best friend's wedding is over I would ask Richard to call her home for dinner but then I could not believe my eyes when I met her at the farmhouse. It was so unexpected, though I knew it was Richard's company taking care of the event and Naina handled the events from the office but seeing her in the room here taking in the notes, I was drawn to her. I was content looking her from behind, she is so beautiful to see. Then on turning she saw me, I swear I saw a hint of smile though instantly she covered it with a frown. Happy she remembered me; my questions got her little confused. I liked teasing her, catching her off guard as I feel those are the moments, when she is not guarding her emotions so well. Again, she was in a hurry to get past me, I felt irritated and did not understand why she has to run away from me. I interrupted her with another of my teasing's I can see she was all flustered. Its spectacular to see her face, each and every expression so clear, her eyes wide and hypnotising I can just get lost in those, as my gaze shifted towards her lips, all I wanted was to kiss her. Somehow, I just had to take my gaze away from her lips and concentrated on what she was saying, it was difficult when she was so close and all confused. After sorting her confusion, when she gave me a big smile I could not stop myself from complimenting her. She looks devilish yet innocent it is a rare combination. Before I could push her against the wall and kiss her senselessly, I decided to leave her there and get back to work. I almost forgot why I was here, she had that effect on me, and it was appalling. Before leaving, I look out of the window. She was taking her night walk I made myself invisible sensing her prior nervousness. I knew she kept her guard up against me and I needed to know. I planned to give her some space tonight so to approach her tomorrow with a fresh start.

The weeks that followed at the farmhouse were quite turbulent between us. Whenever I approached her, I felt she went a little away from me. Until the night when she agreed to come for a walk, that too with much hesitation, I was determined not to let her slide away this time. It was quite a romantic setting; the moment she entered the garden, I lost myself. Under the moon light she looked heavenly, her hair blowing in her face, I knew she was nervous her presence somehow brought a wide grin across my face. It was a very light one, playfully but guarded I answered her question not knowing what would again steal her away from me. One thing went to another and before I knew, I could not stop myself from kissing her. Her lips were so inviting and soft I could not stop myself from getting more. Before I could pull her close, she pulled back. Then ever so slowly fighting the turmoil inside her, she again drifted back to her shell, demanding an answer. I was not thinking straight, so I answered her with first things that came in my head and instantly cursed myself as I could see her retreating. I was very angry with myself and with her for blocking me out again. When she asked me about commitment, I told her what I thought.

I sat on the bench for a long time contemplating what had just happened, at one point of time I could see her melt for me and then she practically ran away from me. I was frustrated and fuming inside, I hate that she was crying because of me. I wanted to run behind her and take her into my arms, soothe her tears but then I thought to give her space, turned and jogged to my room. I was not sure what I wanted right now, all I knew was I have lost the chance yet again. I kept my distance from her, for the rest of the days. I wanted to sort myself out, before I could reach for her again. Though I kept a close look on her, I was looking for the opportunity to approach her again. By her behaviour, it was clear, ignoring me was her top priority but I need to slip in, I could not let her go yet. When I saw her lost in her thoughts near the Mandap, I knew I had to talk to her. Surprisingly after a long time I saw her guard down, I did not want to miss the opportunity, I started by complimenting her work, which was exceptionally done. I have often heard Richard praising her work and how much gifted she was. Her eye for creativity and perfection had changed the whole place in to a beautiful setting. The whole ambience was riveting in its own way yet had the touches of what the bride and groom wanted. I was impressed to the core and fascinated by the look in her eyes. There was tiredness, loneliness yet there was hope. Counting on that hope, I asked her to give us a second chance, to my surprise she agreed. Giving her the space, I saved my number in her mobile, thinking she would understand I want to take it slow but I am interested in taking it forward.

It had been a week since the wedding, I did not receive any call or message from her. I was growing impatient I thought I would give her two days more than I would take matter in to my hand. I was surprised by my behaviour and my growing interest in her. I have met many girls in my life, I have been into flings, pure sexual encounters but with her, it is different. She intrigues me, something in me wants to protect her, handle her delicately yet I want her to be wild and free. Take her against the wall and show her how much I needed her. Lost in my thoughts, I missed when my phone beeped.

I almost tripped when I saw her message, I messaged her back to make her known I am still interested. Tonight we are meeting at her command and her choice of dining was excellent. I took matters into my hand and booked the secluded area in the restaurant. I wanted to spend time with her, understand her and definitely kiss her. The later could wait I thought shaking my head and smiling widely. With that thought, I entered the board meeting I had on schedule. I was relaxed that today I only had to sign few papers because focusing on the agenda would be difficult when I had my mind on making this second chance perfect for her.

I entered the restaurant early, I was restless and on edge. I did not know her favourite flower and ordered every colour or roses available. The moment I saw her entering the restaurant, I knew I made the right decision. She was looking stunning, the short dress filled her every curve and the low cut wanted me to do things to her she could not even imagine. Clearing my throat I got up to give her flowers, which instantly brought smile on her face, I realised I was growing addictive to her smile. The sight of her was so over-whelming that I could not stop myself from giving her a peck on her cheeks, which resulted in a wide stare and then a blush all over her body. With great control, I made myself sit in a chair opposite to her.

CHAPTER 13

Naina

I purposely chose the violet dress I wanted to astound him. The way he was looking at me, I knew my hard work has paid off. I have always been careful with people but with him, I wanted to be different which I still have to figure out. How, I am still suffering from the after math of his peck on my cheeks. My whole body filled with warmth and I knew I was blushing profusely. It was not I was expecting but nonetheless I was pleased with this.

His gaze grew more intense, as if that could happen anymore, it was doing things to my body, which was making me all nervous yet wet down below. Finally, he broke the tension "So how have you been?"

Visibly relaxing a little, I told, "I am doing well". I knew he wanted to know why it took me a week so I told him "I took off and went to meet my family for a week".

I could see his gaze growing soft on me, a lighter shade of blue "hope you had a nice week."

"Yes, totally, Family is the best medicine after hectic months at work".

His smile was back "I agree. Who all are there in your family?"

"I am the eldest and the only girl, I have a joint family". There was pride and love in my eyes as I spoke about my family. He noticed it too.

"You must really love your family, I can see that" I nodded.

At this moment waiter came in with a menu, I realised I was starving but then what exactly I wanted my heart asked food or the Greek God sitting in front of me. I shushed my heart and concentrated on the menu, which was difficult when you have host as sexy as him.

We agreed to order the main course, I think he did not wanted to waste time on food. For once, I agreed with him, I could not take my eyes off his lips.

I thought he caught my gaze, he cleared his throat and straightened himself a little on the chair, pressing my lips together I hid my smile seeing his discomfort. I do not know what happened to me, why I was behaving like this making my desire evident to him. Where was the guarded Naina, I think it's all my mom's fault for gifting me the sexy lingerie and dresses, putting ideas into my mind, which seems difficult to take my mind off now sitting here in front of this Greek God.

Nihal

I was confused what has overcome this girl sitting in front of me. Her intense gazes, her shy smile are driving me crazy. The moment her gaze moved to my lips and the look she gave me, I feel I would combust from the effect literally. I was relieved when she agreed for the main course directly; torture of appetisers was not a good option now.

Clearing my throat, I asked her "What are your plans?"

She looked unsettled, her wide eyes told me she has taken my question very wrong, I clarified again "I meant about the future, your job, how long you intend to stay in Mumbai?"

Giving me her shaky laugh, "I have not sorted it out yet. I came to Mumbai for a change and luckily landed myself with a job. I love my job, the nitty grit ties I think I am just settling in. At least, I am here for another six months".

I nodded "Why did you come to Mumbai, so far for a job?"

Something about my question unsettled her, as if she was contemplating the answer, she took her own time answering and the guarded Naina was back "I just wanted to be independent".

The way she answered, I knew there is more to it. There was something she was hiding and was not ready to tell me. I purposely cut her a slack and changed the topic.

"Tell me about yourself, who is Naina?

I could see she relaxed and we slipped into an ease "Naina is a simple girl, loves to live her life to the fullest, enjoying every moment, loves her family the most and keeps always running into problems." To this, she laughed heartily and I could not stop myself from joining her.

I liked the sound of her laugh, it instantly lift's up the world around. I knew I would do anything to see her laughing like this.

Sobering up she asks, "Who is Nihal?"

I gave her my best smile "Introvert, curious, loves to explore and very passionate". I saw her gaze growing intense on my last word and ever so slowly, she exhaled her breath. The temperature around us seemed to have fallen by ten degrees as we kept looking each other with potent desire in our eyes. Then suddenly she averted her gaze and looked conscious.

"Do you like movies?" she nodded.

"Would you like to go for a movie tomorrow?" with a smile she nodded again.

We ate dinner in silence; I was not ready to let her go, we went for a walk near the beach. Something about her kept me drawing towards her, I saw her face lit up in a mischievous grin and to this, I raised my eyebrow.

Innocently she asked me "do you like water?" I nodded and then I saw a splash of water drenching my shirt. I was taken aback then followed her footsteps running behind her, I was tall enough and it took me few strides to catch up with her. Catching her from behind I took her into my arms with one arm free I splashed water on her. Giggling uncontrollably, she moved close towards me hiding her beneath me. We were breathless from our recent game, I pulled her closer titling her chin up.

Her eyes were soft and tempting I bowed down and closed the gap with a kiss. When timidly her tongue touched mine, I deepened the kiss pulling her tightly into my embrace. My whole body was on fire, moving my lips towards her neck, I licked sucked and bite her skin there. I could feel her body shudder; her responses were so uninhibited. She drew her leg around my hips, bringing our body closer the friction caused us to moan. I wanted to tear her dress away, I knew this was not the place I straightened pulling her into my embrace. I could feel her tremble below me pulling her away a little I cupped her face and kissed again.

I whispered licking her ears "Let's go to my place?" I waited for her response she took time in deciding.

Titling her chin up, I asked to open her eyes, when she looked up I could see confusion, fear and indecisiveness there. Drawing a long breath, I sighed and waited for her response.

Pulling her lips between her teeth with a tremble breath "It's too fast for me, Nihal I don't want to jump in the bed so soon. I want this to happen slowly, want to know you more".

I knew her guard was up, the need to take her was so strong it was unbearable to stay away from her, exhaling a frustrated sigh, I nodded in understanding taking her hands in mine, silently, we walked towards the car. We were quite the whole time, I did not know what to say or react anymore. Dropping her home, I cupped her check, kissed on her forehead and left without any words.

CHAPTER 14

Naina

A new day, a new morning and a new beginning, I have always believed in that. Yesterday night came as a shock of emotions and experience. I wanted to kiss him that what had happened but the moment he embraced and asked me to move to his place, sense knocked in. I wanted to take it slow with him, I did not wanted to be a one-night stand. I wanted to be in control of my feelings and decisions, did not want to take things in the heat of passion. Though I am confused with his reactions, I did not even know whether our movie plan was on or not.

I texted him, "Good Morning"

"Good Morning, beautiful. So what's your plan for the day?"

I was relaxed he replied but then bewildered by his next question, I decided to take it light "I have a movie date with a handsome guy I met last night for dinner".

"Oh! I thought of picking you up for lunch, since you already have plans then maybe next time."

I liked he played along "As I am very understanding and flexible, I can accommodate lunch and then can go for movie"

"Wow, you would do that for me. Wouldn't your date be jealous?"

"Why would he be? I am thinking he is very understanding."

"I hope not, because I am a charmer and won't let you slip away that easily."

My heart skipped a beat "Poor guy, he has to fight hard then."

"Well there isn't a fight I am planning to keep you to myself all day. I hope you won't mind to that".

Damn, he knows how to flirt he makes my heart beat erratically. Even with distance, he can make me feel wanton with his few words, how I will be able to protect my heart from him, I doubt.

I replied, "I don't mind to be charmed by your company all day."

"Be ready, will pick you up in an hour's time".

In an hour's time, that is not good. I am still in my bed, groggy from my sleep. I pull out from the covers and rush to take bath. My apartment is a mess, I need to unpack my bag, need to wash my hair. I decided to go subtle today, after last night anything as sexy as that will definitely lead me to his room I realised, so I took out my only washed and ironed pair of jeans with a long sleeve top which hung perfectly over my breast.

Nihal

Morning with her flirty messages was indeed a nice start. She is a relishing mystery, full of wittiness and playfulness. I was surprised at myself I was looking forward to the day with her. I decided I would take it slow, give her time to open up as I have also seen an unguarded version of Naina and she was more fun to be with. Her smile is more effortless when she is relaxed my heart yearned to hear the sound of her laughter. As my thoughts drift away, I could not stop myself from thinking about the kiss and the way she kissed back. My whole body shivered with the anticipation of another one, my groin went harder at the ways I would like her to come. Shaking my head I headed off to shower to cool myself off and with only one thought in my mind I needed to take it slow with her which I was not sure how to do.

I was waiting for her near her apartment, the sight of her was very captivating, and she looked more alluring than last night. I knew it would take lot of efforts today to keep my hands off her. To satisfy my urge for the time being I hugged her. I realised it was a mistake her perfume was overpowering and it turned me on. Before I could stop myself, I kissed on the side of her mouth, her sharp intake of breath made me feel satisfied. Knowing how her body reacted to my touch will make it more interesting to see her controlled and planned reaction towards me.

Smiling into her wide eyes, "Hello beautiful ready for a ride" Her confusion and nervousness was evident she politely nodded with a shaky smile. I knew, it would be a game of pleasure and teasing which is result would be very passionate indeed. Though she thinks she is setting the rules, she is not even aware I have taken things into my hand.

Traffic in Mumbai is a pain in the ass but today they came as a welcome distraction. Since she was, quite I offered to break the silence "Is your date going to pick you up from the restaurant?"

Baffled she looked at me, I gestured to our early morning messages catching on my meaning with naughty look she said, "I thought you would like to keep me to yourself all day".

Smiling, "I want to see you next to me in my bed all day long".

Though my eyes were on the road, I knew she was nervous, she did not realise how well I have come to know her body and her reactions towards me. I thought to let her know but seeing her all nervous, changed my opinion instead allowed her to change the topic, when she spoke next "Where are we going for lunch?"

"Do you like to go to a restaurant or would you prefer roadside?" I asked her nonchalant, though I wished she would choose roadside, it will give me more time to be with her without disturbances.

"Roadside would be a great idea," she said brightening up. "What's your favourite food?"

"I don't choose between my babies, I am a foodie by heart". She nodded and added, "I agree, I am a foodie too and I love to explore."

"What else do you like to explore?" Giving her my naughty smile, I challenged her with my tone. I wanted to test her limits how much she is willing to give away.

Sweetly ignoring my tone "I would like to explore the whole world, its culture, sceneries, beaches, sports everything that came along". I raised an eyebrow.

She added, "Repetitiveness, following the routine, bores me out, I love creativity, challenges, and pushing my limits I think that's why I love my job. It thrills me to the core." I was impressed.

Parking my car to the farthest corner, I ordered a roll for both of us. It was a quiet Sunday, which is rare in Mumbai, looking at Naina gives me a content feeling, which is rare. I know I like her but to what extent. It has been long since I had a proper dinner date, usually I am busy with business meetings and I had to admit this one would be hard to forget. Generally, I go on dates ending in my room but with Naina caution and slow are the two things, my mind kept on reminding me.

Breeze caressing her face, her hair all flowing, I bend forward and tuck her hair behind her ear, a small gesture but sends shiver all over her body and make my groin tight. I want her badly, lying beneath me, my hands on her breast, my lips kissing her.

Stop… Nihal, no. You will scare her away.

"What are your plans for the week?" I asked drawing my gaze away from her lips.

"I really don't know. Will be joining office tomorrow after a week's break, I have no idea what Richard has in stored for me". Her voice was also making me horny I shifted a little in my seat.

Looking towards me she asked "Is something wrong?"

Yes. I wanted to say. I want to take you home and do things to your body that will leave you breathless.

"No" I shrugged I leaned in and took her lower lip in my mouth. She leaned in too I liked that. Slowly nibbling her lower lip, I traced my tongue over it. I could feel her hands clutching my t-shirt. She moaned and I gave her a full kiss. I took full liberty to explore her mouth the way I wanted. I wanted to appease my hunger, ever so slowly I increased my pressure on her lips, then when I knew I wouldn't be able to control myself I withdrew. She was breathless, bewildered, I smiled I needed her to feel what I was going through. I knew she is going to leave a mark on my heart that thought irritated the hell out of me.

CHAPTER 15

Naina

What was that kiss for? It left me breathless, wanton and panting. What had just happened, I am so confused. When I thought he would take it further, suddenly he left me wanting for more. Nihal not only ruled my senses but my body too that thought terrified me. Every second spent with him is a constant fight between my body and mind. I am consumed with passion, if he wanted he could have taken me here and I would not have said no, the thought annoyed me more. I decided I cannot be timid in front of him he is doing it again, dominating my senses.

I spoke infuriated more on myself than on him "What is wrong with you Nihal. I told you last night we need to take it slow, then why do you keep pouncing on me at every given opportunity."

I knew I had spoken too much, because next when he looked at me I saw anger in his eyes "When did I pounce on you" he said with an ominous voice "What is it you want Naina, haven't I taken you to a respectable dinner and then lunch today. For your information, my dates lead to my bed, if that is what I wanted I would have taken you last night. I am trying hard, giving it a chance."

"I …." I stammered

"You want me to keep my hands off you, not touching you or kissing you. Fine, I won't do it again," he said furiously.

I was quiet, no I did not want that, I want him to touch me, I liked that then why do, I over react. Lost in my thoughts, I did not know how to respond.

Exhaling deep breath "Naina, don't test my patience, I have a thin one. I would not lie to you I want to kiss you. Damn I like kissing you and I want to make love to you. Keeping my hands off you would be very difficult for me. I have never courted girls but I am doing this for you. You need to understand that. You can't close up on me, every time I touch you or kiss you".

I could not speak I shifted in my seat looking outside. What am I supposed to say to this, he wants me in a physical way not in a loving way? That is what all it is about SEX. Am I ready for relationships like this, should I let my heart take the leap and shut my mind out?

Cutting in, exasperated he says, "Say something Naina, your silence is killing me".

"Nihal, I don't know if I am ready for a purely physical relationship. In fact any relationship for that matter." Tears welled up in my eyes I did not know what to say.

"Do you like me? Do you like spending time with me? Do you like when I kiss you?" I nodded.

"Then that's fine. Let's keep it till there. I want to kiss you, take you in arms but I can promise I will not go further until you ask me to. This I want from you and I will take it from you whenever I want, don't close up on me".

He spoke in a very possessive tone, which I did not like but the way he spoke; I did not have courage to disagree so I nodded. Holding my hands in his, "It's difficult for me too, but I want to give this thing a fair chance before we say goodbye". To this, my heart skipped a beat and sadness enveloped me.

Rest of the drive we held hands, as if he was afraid I would bolt out of the car and run away. We went for a long drive instead of a movie. After such a heated discussion and admissions I don't think both of us were in a mood to watch a movie. I was still absorbing whatever had happened between us.

CHAPTER 16

Nihal

What am I supposed to do with her? What exactly I want with her, to take her to my bed or am I expecting something else from her? Why is it so difficult to let her go? I cannot do these dates. Then why am I doing it for her? I have to make a call and I can satisfy myself with anyone I want but lately I consumed with the desire for her. This has to stop; I need to think properly yet in my heart, I do not want to let her go. This feeling is new for me and I need closure on this one soon.

Very casually, I told her "I am leaving for London, next week" I have no idea why I am telling her, all I wanted to know was how she would react to the news.

Surprised she asked "For how long?"

"May be a week or two, depending on the business"

"Will you find time to call or message?" I smiled to this "Naina, technology has really advanced these days, we can email, message and talk on phone too."

Rolling her eyes "What I meant was …. Nothing leave it".

God! She is infuriated and shy, her meaning did not lose on me, she wanted me to keep in touch then why could not she just say it. I prodded her a little "What you meant was?" with a raised eyebrow, I asked.

Fidgeting she continued "Am I allowed, I mean, can we keep in touch with messages or email. If it does not bother you"

What the hell, why would it bother me, did not she understand that I am bewitched with her, that I want her as much as she does? Smiling I told her with a firm look "Naina, you can call, message or email me as much as you want. I am not bluffing here when I am saying that I really want this thing, I want to give it a chance. Please don't doubt my intentions Naina, have little bit of trust in me." She nodded.

After a thought, she asked, "Can you email me your schedule, so I am aware when I can reach you?"

I sighed she still does not understand "Yes, I will ask Andrew to mail it to you". Confused she looks up to me, "Andrew is my PA, he manages my meetings and schedules."

Nodding she continued, "When is your flight?"

"Tuesday night". Quietly she just nodded. I wanted to know what is going in her head.

Parking my car outside her apartment, I titled her chin up, forcing her to look into my eyes "What is it Naina, tell me what's troubling you now?"

For a second I thought she wouldn't reply "I… will you .. I mean" I kept looking at her intently, closing her eyes she said in a rush "I will miss you, I don't know if you have any girlfriend there or should I wait for you. I mean I know it's nothing here but I don't know".

Sliding my thumb across her lower lip, making her look up to me "Naina, for the last time I am telling you, there is no one in my life except you right now. Can you drop this hesitation, worry, whatever you want to call it? Let it go, Naina."

Sighing with my fingers I pulled her lips to mine, touching softly, when her lips parted I traced them with my tongue, savouring her taste. I was getting addicted to her lips and these kisses were dangerous as it made my desire for her uncontrollable. Tearing apart, I whispered against her lips "I will miss you too". I didn't realise I said it aloud, till she whispered "Thank you".

Drawn to her, I almost asked her to accompany me to London along but with much will, I stopped myself, kissed her forehead, and walked her to the apartment with one last look I left. Stunned by my reaction towards her, I have never been soft to any one, and she stirs up some hidden string of emotion in me, which I have yet to understand. Shaking my head, I kept this thought aside and drove back to home.

Naina

Back in my office, meeting my boss feels good. Richard congratulated me for my last assignment. We were having coffee, discussing some re-arrangements when Richard asked me "Have you met Nihal?" catching me off guard, coughing and covering my embarrassment, I told him the truth "Yes, I met him for dinner". I purposely left the lunch part, mentally making a note to message Nihal about the same.

Raising his eyebrow, "So?"

Shrugging I asked, "So?"

Sighing "Naina, I hate going around the bush, tell me the status about your two relationship. Now do not tell me, there is nothing. I have seen you two exchanging looks and the way Nihal talks about you it's quite evident he is fond of you".

I was shocked, when did Nihal speak about me with my boss and what has he told him, are we in a relationship? I did not know what to say, I kept quiet. Thankfully, Richard phone buzzed at that moment, showing me one finger he went to his other room to take his call.

Immediately I texted Nihal "What have you told Richard about us?"

"What do you mean?"

"As in Richard is asking about our status"

"Really" I could sense him smiling and enjoying this.

"NIHAL, stop making fun of this"

"NAINA, I am not". Sometimes it gets difficult to know what he is thinking. Therefore, I called.

"Hello"

"Hi, Naina" Oh yes, he was smiling.

"What does Richard know?"

"About what?"

God, he is irritating "Nihal, what did you tell Richard about us"

"Naina, will you explain everything, so that I know what are you talking about?"

I explained him the whole conversation, laughing he said "Richard is pulling your leg, he loves to do that. We met for dinner last week, very casually I just complimented him for the whole event and how beautifully it was done".

Now it was my turn to be surprised "Really, you liked the décor".

"Really, Naina, I loved your work and I am very impressed. I don't throw around compliments unless someone deserves it".

Self-Obsessed "Thank you". Then I realised I told Richard about the dinner date, to which Nihal was okay about.

Then very casually, he asked, "Do you want us to be secretive about this whole relationship, Naina?" I have not thought about it yet.

"Are we in a relationship?" I asked keeping my fingers crossed

"Well, as far as I am concerned when two people are dating or seeing each other, it is generally termed as they are in a relationship. Do you have any other term for it?"

Smiling, I say, "Okay. It is relationship then." I hear him laughing loudly and muttering, "You are an exception, Miss Naina."

Seeing Richard finishing with his call I bid bye to Nihal and disconnected the call.

As I saw Richard entering he gave me a weird look, I asked "What, why are you giving me such a wierd look?"

"Why are you smiling so much?" I shrugged and contained my smile.

Shaking his head, he announced, "Music and Divine, have opened up a new restaurant and they want us to organise their launch party".

I was escalated it was yet again a big event for the company and definitely, the change I was looking for. Thankfully with me, there were two more executives along, who will be handling the event it would be another thrilling learning experience for me. Richard gave me two days to come up with three ideas for the event, as the company would be coming on Wednesday for the same.

Hearing this I was torn between excitement and sadness, I was planning to give Nihal surprise by meeting him at the airport but presenting three ideas mean I have to sit with my team day and night researching and finishing my ideas into presentation. Urrghhh, it is not easy, as it seems.

After lunch, I busied myself with research and had animated discussions about the event with my core team. My phone was on silent, so I missed Nihal's messages. As soon as we took a break, I read, "What's your plan for the evening?"

"Very busy, have a presentation on Wednesday, working my ass off." I waited for his reply.

"What time will you be free?"

"Somewhere after 11, I guess".

"That's late. Fine I will pick you up by 11".

Dominating as ever, "I have my car Nihal".

"Don't worry driver will drop your car at home. Naina, don't argue with me on this now."

I wanted to meet him too "Okay, will be waiting". Smiling I got back to the conference room.

Sharp 11, Nihal, messaged he was waiting downstairs. Punctual, the quality I admire in guys a lot but then Nihal was always punctual, well mannered, respectful, intense, passionate, strong and I stop myself before I let my mind wander too much.

I met him after ten minutes and I liked when he got down, embraced me in a hug. I was getting used to these hugs mentally I shook that thought away. Smiling I slide into the car. It was very casual conversation, talking about the day. I liked this, if that is what this relationship is all about, I think I can handle it. When we reached the apartment, he smiled naughtily asked, "wouldn't you call me up for a coffee"

Ah! Nihal, the passionate lover, was back I smiled "Its late Nihal".

With a wounded look he says "Where are your manners Naina, I don't think you are interested in me, anymore."

Rolling my eyes, I tiptoed towards him, taking my arms around his neck, smiling into his shocked eyes, I kissed him lightly on his cheeks and then on his lips. When I withdrew he kept me still, close to him our foreheads touching each other. I whispered on his lips "Good Night." We stayed like that for few more minutes, then straightening up but keeping me in his arms he said "Make up your mind, Naina. I can't stay away from you. When I am back from London I want this relationship to take a step forward." I can sense need in his voice. I nodded and he hugged me tightly. Kissing my hair, he pulled me out from his embrace.

I knew it's too soon to say but I would miss Nihal a lot. With that thought, I entered my apartment, changed and set up a reminder to call Andrew for Nihal's flight details. I do not know how will I manage but I need to see him at the airport.

CHAPTER 17

Naina

When you have so much going in your head, sleep eludes you. Therefore, I reached office early. With ideas bursting in my head, I could not pretend to sleep anymore. When my core team joined in, I was ready with spread outs, designs and themes, which we decided on yesterday night. They all seemed relaxed and happy, I was prepared with spread outs and it saves time. Well they were not aware of my hidden agenda to leave office early to meet Nihal.

Gaurav started, "Naina, I was thinking we can start with soft light work near the stage where the musicians are to preform giving it a rustic feel altogether". I like the idea, Gaurav handles the lighting effect in the team. He has a way of making things alive with the right placement of lights. I nodded in agreement and asked Shipra who is managing the stage to plan-out with Gaurav the whole setting.

I knew these were the little details, which could be work out later right now we need to put the whole setting together so that we are finished with the first idea. Everyone handed their notes to Ricky who handles the presentation, he is a computer genius. We all have given our best in the first idea itself. Research is the saviour in these things, we all threw ourselves in the research and were glued to our computers when Richard came to check on our progress. We explained him our first idea, thought he liked it but was not impressed. He needed us to work harder and shared his inputs too.

I felt totally drained out, clock was ticking away. We were not even finished with the first idea. Taking a break, I called Andrew to check Nihal's flight details.

"Hi, Andrew, this is Naina". I was nervous

"Hello, Miss Naina, nice to hear from you". I could feel his smile and of course he knows me.

"Andrew, I need Nihal's flight details and when will he be leaving from office for airport". I gush out.

"Yes, Ms Naina, Sir told me to update you with details. I am hoping you would be joining him at airport".

Oh how I wish "Andrew, here is the catch I may not be able to go to airport but can you deliver my message".

There was a long pause "Umm.. Yes absolutely".

Beaming up, I said, "Great, I will just message you the same. One more thing Andrew please could you deliver it with a flower". I knew I was over stepping the favour.

"Okay". I could hear confusion in Andrew's voice, I think he is doing it for the first time and that makes me smile widely.

Crossing my fingers, I hope Nihal does like my message and understand the whole situation. I still wish of some magic happens and I am able to reach at the airport. What is wrong in wishing at times, I thought sadly.

Nihal

It is been a hectic day at office. Meeting with managers, detailing out work, about this London deal, the company's profit will double. It is been two years I have been working with the London market fighting my space with other brands, after this deal we will be working solely with one of the biggest brands in London. I am happy with where I have taken this company in five years, thrown myself in work, now I want to relax. I wanted to surround with family, happiness, someone to go home with. All these feelings have surfaced within me after I met Naina.

Drifting back to her, her smile, her laugh, being around her makes me feel relax. I hope she is coming to see me at airport though I have not asked her yet. I called Andrew "have you mailed my details to Miss Naina".

"Yes, sir. First thing in the morning" he nodded

"Have you arranged a car to pick her up from office".

"Umm… Sir" He is hesistating, that's not like Andrew. Impatiently I asked "What is it, Andrew".

"Sir, I have a delivery for you from Miss Naina". Delivery from her?

"Come in, Andrew". Andrew carried a letter with a flower for me. That brought smile on my face, Naina made Andrew deliver this. With a raised brow I looked at Andrew, he looked flushed, that is a first time "Miss Naina, asked me to" he explained.

Putting him out of his misery I took the letter and gestured Andrew to leave, then called him to say "Thank you", he shrugged and left. The moment I got the letter I knew she won't be there at the airport, still I opened it.

Dear Nihal,

I thought of surprising you by being at the airport but I think universe loves to play games with me. I am stuck at work, not even through with first idea yet. On second thought, I hate saying goodbyes they make me sad and vulnerable. Anyways be in touch and enjoy you stay. Days will not be same without you here ;).

Hugs and kisses

Naina

Surprised Naina is quite expressive in her letter. She is opening up, this is the very first response from her and it made me smile a lot. I was fondling with a flower when Andrew knocked, "Come in".

"Sir, your bags are ready and in the car. It's time for your flight". Absentmindedly I nodded, took the letter and left for the car.

The whole drive to airport, I was smiling which is not often. Andrew kept giving me looks but did not say anything. How could it be possible that I have not spent a night with a girl still she fascinates me to this extent. I know one thing for sure I want to be in relationship with Naina, the thought itself is very disarming. The next step is taking her out of her closet and making her stay. Something tells me that this would be rather difficult than any of my business deals till date.

I texted Naina "Got your letter, at airport, security check in, will message you when reach". Smiling I send it across I know she would be hassled and after I have not messaged miss you.

When the flight was about to take off, I messaged her putting her at ease "Yup, I will miss you Naina". Laughing I switched off my phone and dreamt about her.

CHAPTER 18

Naina

Lying on my bed, I am thinking about his last message, he knew I would be waiting to hear those words and he deliberately messaged me just before switching it off. God I hate him for this. I decided I am not going to message him anymore. I turned off my mobile and slept.

Next morning, when my alarm clock buzzed, it was five already, I pushed the covers, changed into my yoga pants and went for a jog. Early morning jogging helped me clear my head and it is the much-needed stress buster for days as hectic as today in my office. Forty-five minutes later, I entered my apartment, switched on my mobile. I sulked when there were no messages from Nihal. Going through my laundry, I decided to re-arrange my clothes half an hour later I am satisfied with it, I went for a bath.

During breakfast my phone beeped, I ran for it, it was from Nihal, finally "Reached, driving back to apartment. Thought you would be waiting"

Since I was still angry, I replied "Great".

Instantly my phone beeped "Great, that's it".

"Fantastic, Marvellous, Amazing, wonderful" I texted back

"Now we are talking in synonyms. Naina are you angry?"

"Annoyed, irritated, fuming"

"May I ask why is that so?" Oh! I realised I am stuck in my trap. Why am I angry because he took more than an hour to say I miss you, Naina you are doomed.

"How was your flight?" I did what I am good at, changing the topic altogether.

"My flight was very comfortable, thank you. I am still waiting for your answer to my previous question".

Crap! I thought, he is not going to let it go, its better I answer him anyway, consciously I texted him "because it took you long enough to text me back". I smiled smugly, was happy the way I wrote him the reason without letting him know the real reason.

My happiness is short lived "Text you what back?" agitated to the core. He is one smart man "Miss you".

"I miss you too, naina ☺" he replied with a smiley, he knew all along. In spite of getting angry, I was smiling and my heart did some dance of its own. I knew one thing for sure I am falling for Nihal and that too at a lightning speed.

At office, everything was chaotic. I knocked at Richard's door "Naina, I expected some larger than life ideas from your team. I am very disappointed, please pitch me some good ideas by the end of the day. Come out with something that would be original"

Now it was my turn to get irritated, what is Richard expecting from us. For the first time I do not understand what does my boss really want. I went inside the conference room and my heart just went out to my team when I saw their sullen faces. Calming myself, I spoke "Okay, I know Richard did not like the idea. It is okay. We have the whole day to work out another one. Let us start with this, it is your music launch, how would you like it to be. Let's work on these lines and be back by lunch with our ideas". I saw little glimmer in their eyes, I hope crossed my fingers.

The whole atmosphere in the conference room was tense, Richard mulling over the ideas we have presented to him. In an hour we had meeting with Music and Divine members, I was fidgeting in my seat waiting for my boss reaction. Richard turned to me looked at everyone's faces, ever so slowly his lips twitched "Let's crack the deal". I relaxed; finally, we did something that Richard approves.

Meeting with the company went above than satisfactory. They loved our fresh approach towards the whole event. Shipra presented the whole idea and she was good at it. I was smiling I knew by the expressions on their faces we have bagged the deal. After final inputs and their ideas, they finalised the deal. We were all happy and it was time for celebration.

I texted Nihal "We did it".

"What, when, did you drugged me to sleep".

At first, I was confused and then it registered, Gosh "We got the deal". Ignoring his remark

"Ohhh! Good. Congratulations. So where are you celebrating tonight".

"No not tonight, I am tired, need hot shower and sleep."

"I am good in showers". Gosh, he is in a naughty mood.

I played along "Care to join me. Would you like soap or shower gel?"

"Beautiful, when I am there you won't need any of this". Hot images crossed my mind and liquid heat flowed down my body. Even teasing Nihal is dangerous for me.

Innocently I changed the topic "So how was your day?"

"Meetings, meetings and meetings, though right now I am heading for shower." Ahh! Leave it on to Nihal it's difficult to change topics.

"You enjoy your shower, I will head to home." I thought the conversation is over but Nihal had some other plans.

"This how you treat, the man of your dreams, leaving him alone in a shower". I laughed loudly.

"If I met man of my dreams, I would stick to him like leech".

"Beautiful, believe it or not, I am the man of your dreams. I will make you stick to me like a leech. Just let me come back." I did not know how to reply to this. This man is dominating, stubborn and self-obsessed, how I am supposed to digest that. Then I know these are the qualities, which I have come to adore in him.

CHAPTER 19

Nihal

I waited for her reply, knowing her I knew she would be scared. What I do not understand is she is a very passionate, humorous woman, why does she keep hiding it. I took shower, messaged her again. Somehow, I wanted to continue talking to her so I messaged her "have you reached home?"

"Yes, having dinner".

"Beautiful, what are you having for dinner".

"Mix Vegetables, I am following a diet".

"Diet, you don't need one. As far as I remember, you got the perfect curves. All at the right places." How can she be so naïve about her body, does she not realise she is a very attractive women. The way her curves fill the dresses, it drives men crazy. Hell, she drives me crazy. Another message from her pushes me out of my thoughts.

"Thank you". I can feel smile curving her lips. Another message followed "When are you coming back".

"Are you already missing me?" it took her almost ten minutes to reply. I knew she must have been contemplating whether to open up herself or not. This side of Naina makes me impatient and nervous. It was a relief when her reply came.

"Yes, I am. I know it's only been two days but I am missing your hugs". I was right, she is more expressive in her messages, and I decided to push her a little.

"I am missing you too. What is it that you are so afraid of, Naina?" I knew I would have shocked her by my message. I only hope that she opens up to me. When my phone beeped after fifteen minutes, my whole body relaxed.

"I am afraid of being left alone. I am afraid of letting my heart rule over my mind. I am afraid of where this relationship is going. Most of all I am afraid of being hurt all over again."

Her reply shocked me a little. I knew there is much more to her than she would probably show. I knew it is something related to her past. Above all, I knew one thing I wanted to see her care free, smiling. Most of all I was happy she is letting me in.

Pushing my luck further, I asked "What happened Naina?" patiently I waited. I was aware of my heart beat, ticking off the clock in my room. Every time I pushed her a little, nervousness edges in my demeanour. While I waited for her reply, I opened my emails and started replying them. When I was replying to the last email, my phone beeped. I had not realised, it has been over an hour. I was wondering what exactly happened in her life, the message answer my queries.

"Nihal, I had a steady relationship for three years, my boyfriend cheated on me. Without any guilt or sorry, he just left me. It took me months to realise he was using me for my money. It was not only the money, which he stole from me, he took away my pride, my self-esteem and mentally tortured me by comparing me with other people every single day. Physically he always found some fault with me. It took me months to reach where I am. Hence, I am scared of relationships".

I was numb, I assumed she had only trust issues, but here I see a girl who is shielding herself from the world. Something shifted in me, I felt for her, emotion so strong, I could not identify it. When I see Naina, I see warmth, innocence, love all around her but when she is with me, I see her afraid, confused and isolated. I smiled ruefully, for all the women I have dated and had sex with, I am stuck with a women who has a troubled past. Now the question here is how do I make her trust me and fall in love with me. The realisation that I want her to love me is not that bad, I realised.

With a determination in my mind, I replied, "I am not like him".

Naina

It has been a week since Nihal and I had that intense chat about my past. Though he has been very sweet to me, he kept me updated about his work schedule, he has been very busy lately. The best parts of my day are his morning messages; I think I have become addicted to them. It has been just two months since I met him and already my mornings, nights revolves around him. I am scared to the core, I know I have fallen for him but then I know Nihal does not like to commit. I still remember the night when we first kissed, when I asked him about commitment, the shock on his face was visible enough to let me know he was just having some good time. I knew, it was too early to bring up anything like that but still the question scared him. I groaned loudly in my pillow, why am I thinking about all this. I knew it from the start that I am just physically attracted to me and once his libido is satisfied, I would be non-existent in his life.

Dragging myself from the bed, I forced my way to the bathroom. Was having a lot of ache in my body, I think I must have caught flu or something from office. I looked myself in the mirror the reflection that looked back was terrible. I had red eyes, pale face and my whole body was shivering, I needed to visit doctor but before that I had few important things to finish. Hurriedly I took bath, dressed very casually. When I went to kitchen, I felt like puking at the thought of food, had an apple and left for the office.

One of the most difficult drives I have ever made to office, my whole body was revolting against me, as soon as I reached office, I met my boss, Richard, and his shock expression told me how disastrous I looked. Richard was saying something but I could not understand, suddenly everything around me looked hazy, I hit something, my head is aching badly, I am trying to open my eyes, respond to voices and then I drift off.

I heard some voices, my eyes are heavy, someone is holding my hand, and something prickly is inserted in my right hand, it pains then again I drift off. Slowly I opened my eyes again, there is lot of lights and it hurts, adjusting myself I open my eyes, everything is blur at first, there is a lady standing in white clothes, calling the doctor, in an instant a soothing voice starts asking me questions "how are you feeling?"

My mouth feels dry to speak so I nod my head, I wince as my head hurts, opening my eyes further I see a doctor looming over me. Seeing my shocked face, the doctor explained, "you are in hospital, you were down with high fever for two days. I think you caught some flu".

Sinking in the information I asked for water, gulping down the whole glass I asked "who brought me to the hospital and why does my head hurts".

Very calmly, doctor explained, "I think he is your boss who brought you here, he is very concerned about you, lucky to have a boss like him". I smiled, that I was, he continued, "you fell down on the floor, so there is a little bump on your head, not to worry the pain will go in two or three days." He said with a bright smile.

It was then I noticed that the doctor was fairly smart, he had this million dollar smile which you cannot resist, I slowly eyed him from top to bottom, the doctor likes to work out, his arms were muscular, he seemed to be in good shape and he seems young too. As I looked up towards his eyes, I blushed on seeing that his eyes were on me, he noticed the way I was ogling him, OH NO!, instantly I looked away but not fast enough, I saw how is mouth twitched into a smile. I hate being caught; I suppose I can blame it on medicines later. They must be giving me some drugs for sure, as if the doctor can read my mind he said "You were being heavily sedated, you may feel giddy a little, don't worry it will wear off by tonight but we would be keeping you today at hospital, if your temperature does not return, we will discharge you tomorrow". I nodded

"If you want anything, you can press the button at the side of your bed". I nodded and closed my eyes.

I was waiting patiently for the doctor to leave but it did not happen, I opened my eyes again, it still hurt to open my eyes, I looked up at the doctor, he was looking at me with concerned eyes, I raised an eyebrow, clearing his throat, he asked "Are you fine?"

"Yes, it's just I am having a headache" he nodded and gave me a pill "Don't worry, have this pill, it will help you to sleep". After I had my pill doctor told me that my boss was waiting outside to meet me that brought a smile on my face.

"Oh god, Naina, how are you feeling now?" I smiled and opened my eyes. It was good to see Richard.

With a raspy voice, "I am okay, Richard. Hope you are doing okay?" he looked confused, I explained, "Richard, I left my presentation in middle, hope everything went okay with the client".

He looked exasperated, "Do you think Naina, your health is more important than the meeting. I postponed the meeting and you don't worry about work, the reason I have so many employees is, if someone gets unwell, the others can take charge from them."

I smiled again, Richard has always behaved like a parent to everyone, I asked my next question to the doctor "when can I join office?"

Before the doctor had chance to answer Richard shot me an angry look "Naina, you are not coming to office, till you are fully well".

I countered, "I am better Richard, I will take a day off then I will join. I will not stay at home and get bored"

Richard scowled "No, you are not and that's my order. I am officially granting you an off for a week."

I frowned back at him, I agree my head hurts but the doctor has told me that he will discharge me tomorrow, this means I am keeping better and then what will I do sitting at home for the whole week. I opened my mouth to protest but Richard held his finger and spoke to the doctor, "Did anyone tell her, what condition was she brought to the hospital?"

Sometimes Richard genuinely irritates me, he is treating me like a child, I looked up to the doctor for help but he smiled, obviously, he was enjoying the show. Richard continued, "I was so scared when you just passed out on the office floor, you looked so pale. I am not letting you enter my office until and unless you regain your health." The last line said was in a stern voice. I just kept looking at him, I knew I shocked Richard but then I never knew I would pass out on his floor, I sighed and I was thinking of another way to make him understand that I am feeling better, that I did not need a week's off but then his next line gave me a shock.

He told me "Nihal had called up he was very concerned about you, since you have no one to take care at your apartment, so you will be staying with him". Is he serious, how I can stay with Nihal and why can I not stay with Richard, if he is so concerned so I asked "Why not with you?

"You forget, me and my family are leaving for my friend's wedding for a week" I nodded

I suggested, "I can call my friend to status with me and I am not going to stay at Nihal."

Ignoring my protest, he continued, "Nihal is coming tomorrow, you can discuss with him about your staying arrangements. I am just here to inform you." Nihal is coming back is it already two weeks my mind is racing fast. Why would he suggest me to stay with him, does he not realise that I am not feeling well. Is having sex more important than my health, before I can mull more over these disturbing thoughts, my head start pounding and I closed my eyes.

My face must have shown some emotion, as I was drifting off to sleep I felt someone patted my head and whispered, "Nihal is a nice guy, please let him take care of you. He is genuinely worried about you, Naina". Before I could protest, I was fast asleep.

CHAPTER 20

When I woke up the next morning, I saw someone sitting beside me, I looked more closely again it was Nihal, he looked very concerned and tired. I was shocked, what was he doing in my bedroom, I blinked again, was I dreaming about him. My eyes looked around the room, memories from last night came back. I sighed, I am in hospital, I shifted in my bed and I realised the pounding in my head has been reduced to dull ache. I was tired of lying down, when I shifted to sit up, Nihal suddenly jumped onto my side helping me up in a sitting position.

My whole body reacted to his nearness, my face was blushing and I knew these were the effects of the medicines. I realised I have not taken bath for three days and I smell of medicines, this is embarrassing, when I shifted my head towards Nihal, his smell was very welcoming, all manly and strong. Once I was comfortable, Nihal brought his hands to cup my cheeks, kissed my forehead and asked, "How are you feeling, beautiful?"

Beautiful, I feel so ugly right now beautiful is an understatement to what I feel. I feel all dirty and I smell like an onion, still I muster a smile, "Feeling better". Internally I was accusing God, how can he be so cruel. He could have given me an hour to clean up, dressed before Nihal had to reach me. His next question jarred me from my thoughts.

"Why are you frowning, does your head still hurt?" he checked my forehead with back of his hands for any sign of fever.

I plastered a smile, "Nothing, it's just I have not taken a bath for three days, I smell like an onion, you know you can sit on a chair near the window" I blabbered.

Nihal laughed loudly, I love hearing his laugh, God I am swooning, it is the nicest thing to hear after so many days

"Beautiful, seriously you have been in hospital for three days, down with flu and all you are worried about how you smell." I again started blushing.

Shaking his head, plastering a kiss on my forehead, he went to call for the doctor. Now I am confused, why is he behaving so lovingly towards me as if he cares a lot? On second thought, why is he in the hospital? Where is Richard? Then suddenly I remembered the whole conversation from the night before. I became tense I have to think of a way to wiggle out of this mess. The door opened, the attractive young doctor was back.

With a broad smile, "How are you feeling now?" I blushed remembering, I was glaring at him yesterday and I answered slowly "Better". For a minute I forgot Nihal was standing there, when I looked up I saw Nihal giving me a strange look and was eyeing the doctor suspiciously.

Doctor moved forward to examine my head and I saw from the corner of my eyes that Nihal came closer to my bed, he took my hand in his while he was standing beside me. What was happening, why is Nihal being so protective about me? However, I really liked this side of him.

After examining doctor asked me a few question about the pain, my vision, memory, dizziness, I replied them all politely. Then the doctor went on to Nihal explaining him the medicines to take the time duration, looking at me, "Naina, your temperature hasn't come back and since there is no dizziness or pain anymore, we can discharge you today. I will ask the nurse to prepare the discharge papers. You have to sign a few papers as a part of the formality and then you can leave." He gave me a wide smile, as if I have excelled in one of his lectures.

Further he explained, "I have told your boyfriend about the medicines, please take them regularly, I would like to see you after five days. If you feel any pain or dizziness, do give me a call, my number is there on the prescription." I nodded

Nihal ushered the doctor outside, he was giving some directions to Nihal, I tuned them out as the word *"boyfriend"* echoed in my brain. Has Nihal introduced himself as my boyfriend or has doctor presumed it? Then as if it hit me, Nihal has not still spoken about my staying arrangements. As soon as he entered the room, I spoke "Nihal, I am not going to stay with you". He nodded and ignored me.

Is he not listening to me or has he accepted it. I felt bad, is he not going to argue even once to make me stay with him. I was not expecting his easy acceptance. May be I smelled so bad that he has finally decided not to keep any contact with me. I kept looking at him, he was packing my things, he did not say a word, when nurse came in with the papers, and he silently signed completing all the formalities. Afterward the nurse took me on a wheel chair to his car, by then I was sad.

The drive till the house, he kept silent, I kept looking outside the window. Tears welled in my eyes I did not have courage to face him. I knew now it is all over, I should be happy that he did not argue with me but I was so confused, I blamed it all on the medicines. I thought about the hospital, the way he held my hands while the doctor was examining me, he was concerned about me, wasn't he? Then what happened, why he has not made me stay with him. Why is he taking me to my apartment? I closed my eyes, slide my head backwards, I need to control myself, my emotions were all over the place. As soon as the car came to a halt, I took a deep breath, calming myself before I gave in and started crying in front of Nihal.

The front door opened and he lifted me in his arms, shocked I opened my eyes and protested "Nihal, I can walk, please leave me." I squirmed in his arms, he tightened the hold and whispered in my ears "You are new to my place, let me guide you around my house, once you are familiar with the house and have regained your health, you can walk as much as you want."

It took me time to filter the whole information, my house, he has brought me to his house, I am going to stay with him, I am not at my apartment, as realisation sink in I looked up towards him and saw him smiling lovingly at me. Tears started flowing down, my eyes I could not stop it anymore. Sinking my head in his neck, I cried quietly. Putting me down on bed, he removed the pillows from behind and made me comfortable. He looked up at me, wiped my tears, with a frown he asked, "What happened, Naina?

I was filled with so much relief I could not speak. I sank into the pillows and closed my eyes. Nihal took my hands in his and kissed my palm, waiting patiently for my answer, I knew he would not leave unless I told him what was troubling him, "Since you did not argue with me in the hospital about living arrangements and I smelled bad, I thought you have finally decided to leave me on my own". I told him everything with my eyes closed.

Cupping my cheeks, he asked me to open my eyes, fresh tears welled in them, shaking his head, he explained, "I did not argue because my mind was made up, I did not wanted to fight with you and tire you over this. Naina, the moment Richard picked your phone and told me about your condition, I decided then and there, you will be shifting to my house till you felt better."

He kissed my forehead and then smiled "I will not leave you on reasons which I know I can fix them very easily".

Without thinking, I asked, "Then on what reasons will you leave me?"

He brought his lips closed to mine and whispered "I am not leaving you ever, Naina. You better get used to me hovering around you". He kissed me lightly on the lips and I smiled. He got up and went to the bathroom, leaving me all flustered on the bed. Before I even had time to think what just happened, he came back with a towel "I have filled the bath with warm water" then with a naughty smile, which always takes my breath away he said, "Would you like me to accompany or you can manage?"

I blushed at the thought and refused the offer, he picked in his arms left me in the bathroom, before closing the door he said "I am not locking the door, call me when you are ready". I kept staring at the closed door and then he spoke again "Trust me, Naina, I won't come inside unless you call me. Now please enjoy your bath."

Smiling I took off my clothes and lowered myself into the tub. It felt so perfect.

CHAPTER 21

I never realised that I have become so weak; I was exhausted after a relaxing bath. Changing into boxers and T-shirt, I called in for Nihal. This time I did not protested when he scooped me up in his arms, mentally I was thanking him for letting me stay in his house. As soon as he put me down on bed, I fell in to sleep, vaguely remembering him pulling up the sheets over.

When I woke up, stretching myself I looked over the table for the clock, it was almost twelve in the noon. With a jerk I sat up and a dull ache formed in my head, squinting my eyes I rubbed the side of my head where there was a pain forming. Slowly opening my eyes I realised I was at Nihal's place, no office today, all I am supposed to do is relax and enjoy my sick leave. I remember I have never taken any sick leave from school or work, smiling, I adjusted the bed covers around me and kept lying for few minutes more, regaining my strength.

Roaming my eyes around the room, I noticed there were few photographs on the wall, must be Nihal's family, there was a huge couch near the bed, a bedcover was haphazardly lying on it, may be Nihal slept on the couch. Panic settled in, is not there any other room in the house, there must be, I remember the staircase while coming up but I don't remember anything else. With so many emotions, closing up I never gave attention to the place. Turning my head I saw a beautiful picture of a couple, taking the frame in my hand, I marvelled at the couple in the picture. They looked so much in love and happy. I heard a knock at the door, looking up I saw Nihal with a tray, his smile was so warm and I could not help myself smiling back at him.

He came in set up the tray near my bed, smiling his eyes drifted to the frame I was holding, he took it from me setting it aside the bed table asked, "How are you feeling now?"

Smiling in return, I replied "Better than before". His gaze never left my face, brushing my hairs from my forehead, kissing me there, he settled back towards the tray. "I brought you some breakfast. There's your black coffee, some fruits and a sandwich" thanking him I took the coffee.

There was a awkward silence between us, I asked, "where did you sleep last night?" smiling widely he pointed to the couch. "Why?" I mouthed.

Shoving his hand in his hair, he smiled sheepishly "After you took bath, you just drifted off to sleep, I did not know what to do, I was concerned if the fever comes back, also you did not have anything, what if you felt hungry". He shrugged.

I kept on looking at him, swallowing awkwardly I said "that was very thoughtful of you. Thank you, Nihal." I started nibbling on fruits kept in front of me. Breaking the awkward silence, I asked, "Who is the couple in the picture?"

A warm look crept into his blue eyes, with a smile he said, "My mom and dad". Nodding I asked "Where are they?"

Looking at the picture, he continued, "Mom died through cancer and dad lives in London". I felt sad for him "I am sorry." I did not know what else to say.

Shrugging he said, "It was a long time ago".

"How old were you?"

His eyes were back on me, I could see the sadness in them, I felt drawn to him, "I was fourteen and she had a peaceful death." I smiled reassuringly, though I have no idea what I was reassuring him. I could never imagine myself without my mom she has been the strongest link between all of us. Sometimes when she is out on holidays by herself, we all feel lonely. I think that is what the effect is of a mom in a house.

He shifted his gaze on me, "Why didn't you see a doctor?"

I shifted uncomfortably, because his gaze had a lot of concern and love in them, I answered honestly, "I did not realise I was in such a bad shape and I thought after the meeting, I will visit one."

Shaking his head, he kept his warm gaze on me he continued "Why is it so difficult for you to think of yourself. Naina they are people who care about you and would like you to be safe, is it so difficult to understand."

Dumbfounded I just kept looking at him, "Do you care?" his lips turned into a smile, I realised then I have spoken aloud, I did not want an answer to the question "I .. I am sorry, I just blurted out. You don't have to answer."

With a wide smile on his face, he stood up and sat beside me, caressing my chin with his thumb, sliding it towards my lower lip. My breath caught in my throat, his eyes grew the shade of dark blue, ever so slowly, he lowered his head, just inches away from my lips, he whispered, "I do care for you beautiful and a lot." I fought to stay calm but my body has its own way of showing the desire that was slowly increasing from my stomach and like a storm enveloping my whole body. I waited from him to move but he stayed, opening my eyes I looked into his, begging through my eyes to close the gap, he didn't, he just stayed there, his breath caressing my lips, frustrated I hooked my hand in his hair and pulled him towards me, closing the gap. For a few minutes, he allowed me to ravish his lips, the way I wanted, nibbling on his lower lip, biting it hard. He moaned and I delved my tongue inside his mouth. The moment my tongue touched his, he took control, the kiss grew more passionate, stroking long and deep with his tongue, he kept the assault until we were both breathless.

Our foreheads were touching each other and we were panting, his kisses are the most intimate ones I have ever experienced. They push me to an edge where I want to lose myself totally without thinking about the consequences. With his thumb he urged my chin up "Open your eyes beautiful, I want to see you". Slowly I opened them and I was taken aback by the raw emotions in his eyes. He did not say anything for a long time, just kept looking at me as if he could read what was going inside my head. His gaze held mine my heartbeat had accelerated with every breath I took. He lowered his gaze to my swollen lips his lips twitched "I missed kissing you. I missed the feel of your lips and my tongue tasting them." As if to make sure I believe him, he ran his tongue over my swollen lips, enticing a groan from me. How such a simple act from him can melt my whole body in response.

He moved his tongue on my lips, on my ears sucking my earlobe licking it he whispered "I want you beautiful." At that moment for a few seconds, I forgot to breath. He bit my earlobe harder "Do you want me, Naina?" I could feel my whole body shivering with a need so strong. Before I could mouth yes, his phone started ringing, cursing under his breath he shifted and took the call.

"What?" he snapped on the phone. Then raking his hand in his hair, he mouth the words wait and went out of the room. By the time he left I was shivering, what had just happened? Do I want to go forward with him? My thoughts were scattered all over the place, not sure what to do, I ran towards the bathroom. I ran so fast, I almost lost my control but before I could hit the floor, Nihal caught me.

Holding me from my shoulders, he raised an eyebrow, I fumbled with words explaining him "I..I was feeling hot and I want to take shower, I.. I .. I lost my control." He smiled, kissed my forehead, he said, "Okay, I will meet you downstairs in twenty minutes." Ruffling my hairs and whistling he went towards the door, just before closing the door, he poked his head back and said, "Naina, I want you and I am not letting you ignore this anymore. I know you want me too." winking, smiling he left.

I just kept staring at the door, what had just happened. He had already made the decision and I knew there is no stopping him, this time. I cannot let my emotions rule over me. How long is it been that a man has shown genuine interest in me? What is wrong in enjoying few moments, knowing that someone cares and wants me? I want to feel his hands over my body; I want his tongue exploring me, I want my hands on him taste him and kiss him endlessly. I am tired of denying myself the pleasures, which I think Nihal can give me. All I have to do is to keep my emotions out. I made a deal with myself, I will enjoy the time with Nihal without getting my emotions involved. Once this is over, I will find a way to cope. For now, I am all yours Nihal, smiling with a resolve I went to take shower.

CHAPTER 22

The whole day went in a blur. After shower, I went down to see him waiting for me near the dining room. My heart skipped a beat, he too had taken shower and was wearing T-shirt, a low waist jeans. He was looking ruggedly handsome. When he turned his head, he caught me gazing at him my whole face covered with red, immediately I looked down. Smiling he came forward, with his thumb under my chin he brought my face up and said, "I like it when your cheeks turn pink."

My heart stopped beating at that exact moment. He brought his lips closer to mine, "Breathe, Naina." Brushing his lips on mine, he took my hands and took me for a tour of the house. Slowly exhaling each breath, forcing my heart to beat steadily, fighting with emotions clogging my mind, I went along with him. Right now, I could have gone anywhere he would have asked me to? As he showed me the house I kept looking at him with awe, the house was beautiful. It was a two-storey building the ground floor had the kitchen, drawing room, library and a pool. Perfect place for parties, bonfire evenings, the first floor consist of four bedrooms, huge with their own closet and bathrooms.

I realised his room was the biggest of all, the one where I am staying. I thought it was a guest room, but when he mentioned it was his room, my cheeks turned pink again. Now I understood why he slept on the couch. After the tour, we went and sat in the garden near the pool. He told me it was his favourite place in the house. We sat there, both lost in our thoughts, as he lie down on the benches relaxing, soaking the sun, I was just happy laying there as my body still felt weak.

I never knew silence between two people could be so comforting at times. For once, I was not worried about us, about what does he think about me, about our future? I was just happy he was there for

me taking care of me, letting me relax. It has been long since anyone has taken care of me and I felt loved. The whole time when he was showing me around, he held my hands, at times when he was sharing some memory of his, his fingers brushed my hair from my forehead lightly. He kept looking at me with a smile, brushing his lips over my hand every now and then.

Nihal nudging with his shoulders, asked "Penny for your thoughts?"

I laughed what should I tell him, I am happy and loved. On the other hand, should I tell him I have fallen hard for you? OH MY GOD! I have fallen for this man sitting in front of me, staring at me intently waiting for an answer. I looked up into his eyes and I felt the ground slipping beneath me.

NIHAL

I look at her confused, one moment she was smiling, laughing enjoying herself and the next moment her eyes goes wide with surprise, I see a lot of emotions flicker in those beautiful big black eyes. I wait patiently for her to reply, but I see her lost in her thoughts. Something is disturbing her, as if she realised something, which she is not ready to accept. As usual, she is fighting her emotions.

I pressed her hands lightly, letting her know I am waiting, she gives me a blank look, I asked her again "What are you thinking, beautiful". She closes her eyes for a minute and when she opens them, I knew I lost her, her wall is back, with a forced smile she says "Nothing much. I enjoyed the day with you". It took all in me to smile back to her. Why does she have to fight so hard to be happy? I purposely let the topic drop for now on.

"Would you like to play scrabble?" I could see relief in her eyes as she nodded in response.

As we walked into the library for the game, I explained her "Scrabble have always been our family game. When I was small, mom used to say if I need to improve my vocabulary then this is the game we should play every weekend."

Giggling, she says, "Do you mean you suck at words". I love it when she brings humour in small things I say. Winking I replied "Yes, I love to suck but not at words beautiful, I challenge you, if you win, you can ask me any favour and I would do."

I could see her eyes twinkling with mischief already "Anything", I replied "Anything. What if I win?"

Smiling, she said "No chance. I have been playing scrabble since I was nine."

Pouting, I said "What if I do?" her brows wrinkle as if she is thinking hard and then making up her mind, she says "If you win, you can ask me anything you want".

Smiling, I replied "Deal". I already know what I am asking her, winking and kissing her forehead I lay down the game on the table.

We played for over an hour, had enjoyed every bit of it, it filled me with warm memories of the afternoon's I used to have with my mom, it's her last chance if she makes the word and score the point, I would be in deep shit. I underestimated her she is good. I am surprised, how many things are common between us, how much relax and light I feel when I am with her. Looking at her making her smile makes me happy and content man. When I came to know she was at the hospital, I realised that my feelings run deep for her.

In a short span of time, she has managed to capture my heart and these few days spent in her company just confirm how much I care about her. Though I need to know, how does she feel about me, is she ready for a relationship?

Waving a hand over my face, she asked, "Hello, where are you lost. Will you do the total?" She is nervous I smiled at her and started calculating the scores. Stunned I looked up at her, seriously, she did it. She won the game.

She raised her eye, wounded I replied "You won". For a moment, she kept looking at me and then she got up, started dancing all around the room. I could not stop laughing this was hilarious. Laughing she lied on the couch, smiling I got up and hovered over her. Seeing her so happy, I could not stop myself, I wanted to pull her close and kiss her senselessly. Taking my shoulders as support, she tried to sit up but in turn, she pulled me closer. The moment her body touched mine, my smile vanished, my hands automatically went up her neck and pulled her close. I kissed her passionately, she opened her lips for my tongue and my whole body jerked to the sensations.

Her hands are in my hair and pulling me closer, my hands travel down her back near her hips and I jerk her body forward, her breast pressed against my chest. I tore from her mouth and start nibbling her jaw, moving towards her ears. I can hear her ragged breathing, I want to tear her clothes away and take her on the spot but I need to know, if she is ready. "I want you, Naina. Please say yes."

I bit her earlobe and her whole body shivered, I move down to her neck, kissing her throat, biting her neck, sucking at the spot and then licking again. I could hear her moan, so I repeated the whole thing again, I wanted to leave my mark on her. Slowly making my way up, I kissed her again, this time I took my time, nibbling, biting, stroking her slow with my tongue. I tear my lips and look into her eyes. Her eyes are filled with passion I could see she wants me. I want to hear her say the words. "Baby, please say yes".

"Yes, Nihal"

"Are you sure, love" I was excited, but I wanted to make sure. I do not want her to regret it.

"Yes, Nihal. Please."

I kissed hard again on her lips, then carried her to my room. I wanted to make it special for her. I have never been so happy yet afraid. I could hear my heart beating fast I am going to make wild love to her all night.

CHAPTER 23

Naina

I felt warm as I opened my eyes, I saw Nihal sleeping beside me. His one arm is over my stomach and my legs entwined with his. Last night was incredible the fact lies in the sore muscles am having today. I never knew making love could be so beautiful. He is insatiable we did three times, when finally sleep took over us. I blushed when I remember how loud I shouted his name when he made me come again and again with his fingers, his mouth and then when he finally joined himself with me. He took his time exploring my body, finding spots that made me moan I never knew Nihal could be so attentive lover in bed.

In my previous relationship, Dhruv never paid attention to my satisfaction it was always about him. About satisfying his needs, his demands, I never knew I could orgasm so many times. When Nihal went down on me, I was so shy and apprehensive about it. But then his compliments, his eagerness to make love with his mouth, won over my hesitation and the way he made me come, I never imagined I could experience orgasms through mouth too. It was all new experience for me. I have no idea where our relationship goes from here. Would he like to do it again or is his appetite satisfied with me now.

He stirred, moving his head from my chest, he looked into my eyes, he looked so handsome, my heart stopped beating, shifting himself he kissed my nose and whispered, "Good Morning, beautiful". I smiled and formed the words morning, I did not trust my voice at that moment. Rolling over he strode towards the bathroom. I stared up at the ceiling not knowing what to do. Should I get dressed and leave for my apartment today. What does this say about us, our relationship? God, why relationships in my life are so complicated. I pushed myself from the bed, collecting my clothes, start changing into them. I was nervous and wrecked by the time Nihal came out.

Forcing a smile, I went towards the bathroom, when his arms slide around my waist and pulled me towards him "Naina, why are you nervous". How can he read me so well, do I wear my emotions on my face?

Again forcing a smile, I lied, "No, I am not. I just want to go to bathroom."

"Naina, don't lie to me". He dipped his head on my neck trailing wet kisses there.

I shivered but did not respond to him.

Biting my neck hard, he whispered "Beautiful, are you having second thoughts about last night."

Sliding over in his arms, I replied "No, Nihal. I had the best night ever."

Smiling he nodded, "Then why are you so nervous. What is going on in your head? Speak to me, Naina"

Should I tell him, ask him, I am afraid what will he say. Will he think I am getting clingy, or is it asking too much from him? Last night was amazing, but what now? I was so nervous I started biting my lower lip.

Nihal, pulled my lower lip from my teeth, "If you don't stop biting it, I will drag you to bed and will make you scream out my name again and again till you beg me to stop." Red covered my cheeks. I smiled and relaxed a little.

Kissing my lips gently, "Beautiful, please tell me what is troubling you."

It is difficult to concentrate, when he is so close, his lips inches away, I blabbered whatever came to my mind "Nihal, I am nervous because…"

"Yes" he dragged his lips to my jaws, leaving trail of kisses behind, moving towards my earlobe, nibbling it.

My breath caught in my throat, I needed to think hard, "I … I don't know what is it between us. What does last night mean … Should I leave or …. stay" He bit my ear hard, sending shivers down my body.

"Do you want to leave, Naina" his voice a whisper, I needed to concentrate hard, to what he was saying. His lips were driving me crazy. He moved his lips towards my throat, nibbling the sensitive spot, biting, sucking it. In between nibbling he asked again "Do you want to leave, Naina, answer me beautiful."

"No. Not when your lips are driving me crazy".

His hands went to my hips drawing me closer to his body, the sensation of our body pressed intimately was so overwhelming. Pulling at my hair with other hand, he tilted my neck for better access slowly his mouth came to my lips "Look at me, open your eyes". I did, his eyes locked on mine, he asked, "What if I am not kissing then, will you stay."

He asked will you stay, is he asking me to stay, my mind is mush right now. His eyes filled with passion and lust, for me. I asked, "do you want me to stay."

"If I say yes, will you stay?"

Bringing my hands towards his chest, I pulled myself away I needed some distance to understand what he was saying. I looked into his eyes, confused "What do you mean, Nihal?"

Taking my hands in his, "Naina, I want you all to myself. I want us to be together. I want you to be my girlfriend. Will you be my girlfriend, beautiful?"

I could not breath, I was shocked, elated, both at the same time. Nihal wanted me to be his girlfriend. He wanted to be with me. He wanted to be exclusive with me. I look up into his eyes, there was sincerity, depth and longing for me to say yes. Grinning, I pulled him close to me and gave him a kiss.

Smiling, he asked "is that a yes"

I giggled uncontrollably, I shouted, "Yes, yes, yes."

Laughing he pulled me close, nibbling my lower lip, he said "let's close the deal, on the bed." My breath caught in my throat, he carried me over his shoulder to his bed.

Looking into my eyes, slowly he started undressing me, there was so much love and warmth, "God, you are so beautiful", as he cupped my breast in his hand and started playing with my nipple. I arched back, pushing my breast into his hands. Watching him lowering his mouth to my nipple, flicking it with his tongue, tracing it, biting it hard with his teeth "Nihal" I moaned. He went to my other nipple, started playing with it and biting it hard. Moaning I lied down on the bed, he kissed between the valley of my breast, going down towards my stomach, biting my belly button, shivers ran through my body.

My hips started squirming below him, "Patience, love. First, I am going to make you come with my mouth." Moving his lips down, he kiss my mound, "Nihal, please". Slowly he spread my thighs wider trailing his tongue close to my wet folds. My hips jerked up, my whole body tensed, sensing he said "Relax, baby. Let me make love to you. Don't close up on me". I focused on relaxing my nerves, but his tongue was playing with my folds, his teeth biting my clit, it was hard for me to relax. "Please, Nihal" I wanted release so bad, the way his mouth was playing with me, making me come close to my orgasm. "I am close" I moaned again.

"Are you, baby" he blew near my sensitive clit and my body buckled up in sensations beyond my control. I shouted "Nihal, please". It was torturous, I was so close yet I was so far from reaching my orgasm. Trailing kisses, he came up to my lips and kissed me hard. Holding his face in my hands, I whispered "Please, nihal, make me come". Stretching himself over me, he reached for side drawer for condom, opening the packet, he rolled it over his dick. Once more, he kissed me, this time his kiss was slow, gentle, filled with tenderness, lowering himself towards me, dragging his dick over my folds. I wrapped my legs over his hips, pulling him closer he looked into my eyes smiling. God, he was playing with me, the more I arched my hips up, the more he played with my folds, frustrated "Nihal, now" I shouted.

Smiling he said "Say you will never leave me."

"I will never leave you." I wanted him to fill me up. I wanted him inside me.

"Say you are mine" He positioned his cock near my opening, my body shivered, I want him to push inside me.

"Please Nihal. I beg you please." I was restless, my whole body burning with desire. Slowly he moved his cock inside, halfway inside he stopped, I shouted in frustration.

"Naina, say you are mine". I was so frustrated with the need I glowered at him and hissed through my teeth "Yours".

With this, his slammed his cock inside me and I moaned his name loudly. It was the best feeling ever. Again he withdrew, pushed harder, every stroke pushed me to different heights altogether. He was not at all gentle, his strokes grew harder and insistent. I gave him what he wanted, matched his strokes by pushing my hips up, there was almost an animalistic feel to the whole sex. Orgasm I had moments later, blew my mind, it felt my whole body shattered into million pieces, after few more strokes, shouting my name he came hard inside me.

He sprawled over me covering my whole body, dropping his whole body weight; I tightened my arms around him, keeping him close. After such an intense orgasm, we both needed time to recover. When our breaths laboured, he shifted his body, kissed my forehead moved over me lying on his back. He discarded the condom in the dustbin and turned to pull me closer. I slapped his hands away and gave him a disgruntled look "What the hell was that?"

In spite of my protest, he pulled me closer "That in my language is called sex". Colour filled my face, "I know. I mean the… the whole … waiting thing." Shifting my hair aside, kissing my neck, he said "I was closing the deal. We are together now, beautiful" the tenderness in his voice, took most of my anger away. Entwining my finger with his, I moved over, kissing his lips, I told him "Yes, we are together".

He hugged me, stretching over he checked time on the watch, then cupping his hands over my face "as much as I want to continue another round, its 9 already and I have a meeting at 11". Blushing I said "okay".

Nibbling the fruit in my hand I was having for my breakfast, I looked at Nihal, in his Navy blue suit he looks like a Greek God. Oh! I know i am exaggerating but then he totally fits in the frame of my Greek God. Shifting his cereal bowl he asks "What are your plans for today?" looking up from my breakfast I answer, "I am thinking of leaving for my apartment today…"

"No."

"What?"

"I said No. You are staying here."

"But Nihal, I am feeling better now and I need clothes to change." I was feeling a little shock and uncertain about his reaction.

"Hmmm… Give me your apartment keys, will sent the maid to bring your clothes here."

Annoyed I speak "I am not letting some maid touch my private things. By the way, why I cannot go to my own apartment? Why do I need anyone's permission for that matter?" I just hate it when someone tries to control my actions. I am not ten years old anymore.

Calmly he spoke, "Naina, I am not ordering you around, I am just giving you an option."

Taking a deep breath, calming myself I spoke, "Really, because that looked like ordering to me. Since we are discussing this, I need to make one more thing clear, I want you to speak to Richard and convince him that I am joining office tomorrow."

Raising an eyebrow, he speaks "Why would I do that?"

Smiling sweetly, I answered, "Well do you remember, I won the game last night."

Snorting, he said "Fine I will ask Richard but in turn you will be staying here for this weekend."

"Wait a minute we are not doing any bargain here. I won fairly and I get the reward. I am not staying here."

He stood up and walked where I was, blocking my exit with his hands, he spoke in slow tone "Why are you being so difficult. What I am asking is for you to stay this week with me. What's wrong in asking my girlfriend to stay with me."

When he says the word girlfriend and the way he says it, my stomach starts fluttering. What I wanted was some time alone, to figure out my feelings. Already it is hard for me to coherent the fact that I have fallen in love with this Greek God and now after being so intimately close to him, I am paranoid of making a fool of myself. I know he cares for me, he has been gentle towards but he does not love me. I need to be strong for the moment when he decides to leave me alone. Oh! God just the thought of him leaving is stifling me to the core. I am going to lose it all, I cannot be a fool again, I cannot know another man how wrecked I would be. I need to run away from him, the overpowering emotions are suffocating me.

Nihal shook me from my trance, worried he asked "Naina, what happened? Why do you look so pale?"

I look into his eyes, but could not form anything in my mind, I just pressed my hands into his chest, moving him away, I whispered "Nothing."

"Beautiful please, don't shut me out" When I look into his eyes I can see the pained expression but I could not bring myself to react. All I need is some time with me alone.

"Please let me go to my apartment." Ignoring his pleas, I begged him.

Raking his hand through his hair in frustration, "Fine, driver is waiting outside. Naina, I want you back tonight here with him". He said with a glare, which clearly told me he would not take no for an answer.

"Okay. Thank you". I dashed out of the kitchen, stopping only to take my purse from the cabinet I could not look back and see his pained expression anymore. The moment I sat in the car, giving driver the instructions for my apartment, I exhaled a huge breath.

One thing I am sure of is that I am in love with my blue-eyed Greek God.

CHAPTER 24

Nihal

Standing in the kitchen, I felt a storm growing inside me. I cannot understand what have I said that triggered such a reaction from her. I was happy that she let me in, went a step ahead with me. The sex was amazing and for the first time I enjoyed having it with her. I loved her shy smile when we got up in the morning I loved when she writhed in pleasure below me. I loved when she shouted my name when she had her Orgasm. Hell, I loved everything about her. Is it so difficult for her to understand that I love her? Then why did she closed herself in the morning, is she regretting the sex or us. If I remember, she loved the fact I called her my girlfriend.

Why is it so difficult to understand women sometimes? I need my head to be clear on this matter, before I do something else to screw this. I really liked Naina and I want her in my life, I want to make love to her every day, I want to go out on dinners with her, take her for shopping, sleep cuddling her, with time, I want to marry her. How am I supposed to do this, if she keeps shutting herself? I need to find a way to keep her with me, this time I will not let her shut me out. Slowly she has become an important part of my life. I need to talk to my dad about it. The only person, who can save me from screwing the only relationship, in my life.

First, I need these meetings to get over with.

Naina

dThe Drive to my apartment helped me in clearing my head. After changing into my clothes, the first thing I did.....

I picked my cell, I called her, after few rings, she answers "Hi mom".

"Hello stranger. Where have you been? It is been a week since I heard your voice. What's going on?"

Leave it to my mom she will come straight to the point. I told her everything from my drive to office, to hospital, to Nihal's house. Of course, I left the amazing sex part aside. However cool my mom is, I am sure I am still not comfortable in discussing my sex life and positions I had with my new boyfriend. Thinking about it, makes me blush from head to toe. Silently, I thank the universe that I am having this conversation on phone with mom, because if she would be here it would be difficult to hide the constant blush from her.

"Naina, what are you afraid of, beta?" my mom soothing tone brought me back to the conversation we were having.

"Mom, somehow I have fallen in love with him and I am very scared".

"Beta, if you are scared of getting hurt, then you should know that every relationship brings pains along with it. You have to take that risk in life."

"I know mom but what if he is fooling around and what if he leaves me alone when he is bored."

Sighing my mom continued "Beta, if he was fooling around with you he wouldn't have called you his girlfriend. He is giving this relationship a name I think by that he means he wants you to be in his life."

"But…"

"No Naina, you cannot let fear rule you anymore. I think you should give him a chance. What if, Naina he is the man you have been looking for all your life. Would you be able to live, by not giving me the fair chance he deserves? Beta, you cannot let past affect your present. What you had with Dhruv was a mistake and I am happy you are no longer with him."

Surprised, I asked, "Mom you loved Dhruv, not once in our relationship of 3 years you discouraged me from meeting him."

After several minutes of silence, sighing she said "I am sorry Naina. I should I have told you this earlier, that I never liked Dhruv. I always thought you deserved much better than him. I never had the courage to tell you the same, I was afraid you would think I am intervening in your life. Stubborn as you are you would not have appreciated my meddling in your relationships."

Contemplating on whatever she said, I agreed that she is right I was blindly in love with Dhruv. If she had interfered, I would have shut her down from my life. After all mom knows how my brain works and I am thankful to her for letting me make mistakes and then standing by my side when I am learning from them.

Smiling I said, "It's okay mom. I understand. Seriously, mom you still believe Nihal deserves a chance."

"Beta, you have always listened to your heart, I have never stopped you. I have never raised you to be afraid of chasing the one you love. If you believe Nihal is the man for you, then I don't want your fears to stop you."

I nodded and then realising she cannot see me "Okay. Mom."

"Naina, it's easy to read romantic novels and spring ideas into your head, now it's time to create your own." With that, I know my positive mom is back on the line.

Smiling I said, "Thank you mom. I love you."

Mom being mom will not let me bid her good bye until and unless, she have given enough instructions to take care of me and then embarrassing me more when she brought safe sex in the conversation. These are the times I realise why cannot I have that much courage to just snap my phone shut but then I knew if I do that, she will call me back make me realise my mistake and then she will give me one of her most boring lectures. Well she may sound cool but at the end of the day she is a mom, cannot help it.

I feel determined after talking to mom I needed the reality check after all. I don't know whether Nihal loves me or not but I know for sure he cares a lot for me. Otherwise who would cut short their business trip just to make sure I am doing okay at hospital. Then made sure to take care of me at his house and last night when he made love to me, he was careful of my health, my needs and desires. Then he seals the relationship with announcing me as his girlfriend. I feel guilty for reacting the way I did in the morning. Even after my weird reaction, he made sure I come back to him. Who am I to joke, his actions itself are more than clear that he does care about me a lot. I decided I am going to give space to Nihal to come to terms with his feelings for me I am not going to freak out anymore. I will take whatever he gives me, because love is giving not taking. Already he has given me so much and all I have done is to shut him out, hurt him in the process. I will not do this anymore.

My phone beeped, smiling I pulled out thinking it would be nihal but my smile faltered when I saw it was my boss Richard and after few seconds my smile returned back because I know Nihal must have spoken to Richard. Since he has kept his word, I thought I would do something special for him. Mentally I made a note to message him after I had convincing conversation with Richard.

All I know now is I want to make this relationship my happily ever after.

Nihal

It is been a hectic day, meeting took more than my time I wanted to give them. As soon as I came out of the conference room, I told Andrew to get dad on line. It's already three in the afternoon, I want to talk to dad before it gets late in London and he leaves for one of his card's night there. Few things my dad is very particular about is he always in office before his employees, he leaves office by five in the evening and night he spends with his few close friends playing cards.

My father have never imposed any rules on me expect to be punctual and be ruthless in meetings. He is not to be as soft at heart but after mom's death, he has never been strict with me. In fact he has made our relationship more of a friend than father and son. Till today, if I am stuck at anything I would always go on to my dad for advice and he has never been judgemental about me. since mom and dad had a very close relationship and theirs was love marriage, I think he would help me in clearing my mind.

My phone buzzed in my office, a very strong and firm voice greeted me at the other end of the line "Hey Dad, hope I am not disturbing your tight schedule".

Surprised at my formal tone, he spoke "What's wrong Nihal, is the London office giving you hard time. Let me know I will pull some strings and the contract will be yours".

Laughing and shaking my head "Dad I can handle these meetings. Have some trust on me."

"I have full trust on you, that's why I have left it all in your hands, son. Still you know if you need any favour all you have to do is call."

Smiling into the phone "I know dad. Thank you. I have not called for business it's a little personal dad."

I paused, not knowing how to start, his concerned voice came "What is it son?"

"Dad, I think I found what I was looking".

I could feel my dad smiling on other end, "So finally, Richard managed to get my son hooked. Is she the same girl, the one who works in his office."

Shocked, I asked "What do you mean Dad?"

Laughing he told me "Oh! You know Richard, for a few months he has been after my life, about a girl who works in his office, how she is perfect for you. I warned him that you are not interested with the big contract lying ahead. I guess Richard was quite intent on you meeting this one. Then when you shortened the London trip, I got a little curious and spoke to Richard about it. He sounded very happy though."

Laughing and a little annoyed I asked, "Why did you not call me"

Sighing he said "I know you son, when you are ready, you will tell me everything but I was not expecting a call so soon. So what's the problem?"

"How did you know there is a problem? Oh! Forget it I don't even want to ask." I went on to explain him about how I feel and what happened in the morning.

"Son, you need to relax. See, you have to understand women are very emotional. I remember it took me two months to convince your mom that I truly loved her. All you need is to woo her and give her space. Through your action, make her believe you really love her. I am sure, she will come around."

"So all I need is to take her on romantic dinners and give her gifts."

Sighing my dad said "Nihal I never took you to be so dumb for my son, spend time with her, make her feel special, this would do to win her heart."

"I will dad." Raking my hands through my hair, I promised more to myself "I will dad".

"Don't worry son, I know you would. Once you get your mind to something, I have never seen you failing at that." After several seconds pause, he continued. "Son, are your sure about her?"

Smiling I replied, "I am very sure dad."

Smirking my dad replied "I never thought I would ever see you settling down. After you mom's death you threw yourself so much in to studies and then work. I worried whether you will stop and relax, have time to appreciate life. I am happy that finally you have decided to open up and enjoying the beauty of the life. I am proud of you son."

"Thanks Dad". I knew my dad worried about me, but he never showed his concern. He has seen me buried in something or the other, as this was the only way I dealt with the pain and loss of my mother. Since Naina stepped into my life, I have started smiling again, have started seeing life in a different perspective, I feel that emptiness filling up. I feel hopeful toward life, I want to stop and enjoy life. I want the warmth, care, love which have been missing from my life from a very long time. I want Naina to fill the missing pieces in my life with her love.

As if on cue, my phone beeped and there is a message from Naina "I reached our home and let me know what time you will be reaching☺". Seeing her message relieved me…. Our home has a nice ring to it. I am happy Naina is out of the black mood, which she was in the morning.

I messaged her back "Will be back by 7". Through intercom I buzzed Andrew to come, asked him to arrange for a bouquet of flowers and get it delivered my house at 6pm.

Smiling to myself, I knew it is a new leaf in my life. The one that I am going to fill with love, care and laughs.

CHAPTER 25

Two Months Later ....

Life has been good to so far. I never thought I would find someone who would love and cherish me and would accept me the way I am. After the call with my mom I went back to Nihal's house, though I prefer calling it ours, I made dinner for him. I know that's quite stupid of me but what the hell, I love him and I want to make him feel special. Surprisingly, I realised I do love cooking for him. The whole experience gave a new meaning to my life.

Nihal was surprised and pleased that I cooked for him, we enjoyed our dinner, we discussed our day, it was all so natural. When I surprised him with a cake, he could not stop himself from devouring me with kisses. I love the kissing part more. He confessed that he missed homemade food after his mom died. Silently I promised myself that I would make sure we have dinner together. Oh! I almost forgot the flowers he bought for me. My Greek God is romantic too!

We spent the weekend with loads of sex, I never knew we could do it in so many positions few of them were as difficult as mountain trekking. I am happy that Nihal, is open to suggestions not only in life but also in bed. He loves to experiment, bed experiments leave me breathless but when it comes to his cooking experiment, we always end up in take away. So it is a clear rule I do the cooking and he'll do all the wooing, which I think is not a bad deal at all.

As suggested by Nihal weekends I stay with him, now I also have my own cupboard in our house, few weekdays he comes over at my apartment. Though he is constantly begging me to shift to his place but I keep refusing him. I am still scared what if one day he decides it is enough for him, then, at least I have a place of my own to go back to. I know this is silly but my logical part compels me to do this. I won't say Nihal does not irritate me, sometimes when he becomes too controlling, it gets on my nerves. These are the times I am happy I have a place to go and hide from him. I am still working on my trusting issues but I have come a far way from it.

My friends are happy that I have a doting boyfriend after whatever I have gone through. They love him, why not when he makes me so much happy in life. With Nihal I do not have to explain my desire to work, to space out sometimes and to freak out. He always understands me. When our schedule becomes hectic, we keep in touch through text messages. Like today, is very hectic for Nihal, the first order of his London-deal is ready and he is making sure the whole order is packed according to the instructions of the company. My schedule lately has been very easy going, Richard has hired a new team of employees, my job is to train them. It becomes a little less hectic when you don't have to do the field work. Taking the liberty of being the head, I took an early off. I thought of making Chinese, our favourite food.

Since Nihal has been having late nights from last two weeks, I decided to start our weekend a little early. With table ready with candles, food almost prepared, I want to surprise Nihal and make his evening relaxing and playful. He should be there any minute.

When my phone starts ringing I ran across the room, thinking it's another call from Nihal informing me he will be late again, without looking at the caller, I swiped the green button, "Don't you dare tell me, you will be late again", I fumed.

After few minutes' silence, the voice echoed, "Naina….", I am trembling to the core.

Nihal

These two weeks have been really hectic, I am happy now I can leave office. I am exhausted, all I need is to cuddle up against Naina and doze off peacefully. Looking at my watch, I slide into my car, it's already past one. I am thankful Naina is staying at my place it makes things easier. I still don't understand why she can't shift to my place, what is holding her back. I have tried explaining, arguing, forcing rather everything in my control to make her shift but she would not budge. I decided to give space, since she is so adamant about it.

I love having her around she has filled my life with so much love I could not fathom. These two weeks have been the worst, I have been moody beyond reason, have cancelled our dates, with work pressure I am not able to give her time which she needs. Not once have I seen her complaining, she has been like a rock solid support throughout the way. There are times when she freaks out and spaces out, they are frustrating as hell, but when she comes back, I see her coming back with more trust than before. I usually allow her to take maximum of two days to shut me out after that I take control. I admit those two days though happen once a month but are the hardest for me to continue. She is like that fresh breath of air that keeps me intoxicated all the time. She is my own personal drug.

Finally, I am home, I enter the house its eerily quiet inside. Exhaling heavy breath, I move further, its dark I call out to her but there is no sound. Slowly I enter the patio and I am stunned. The whole patio is alight with candles and roses around, inhaling the fragrance I move forward. Dinner is kept on table, I feel annoyed with myself, again, I have killed her surprise by being late. I look around for her and there she is my beautiful princess, her back is towards me, not missing an opportunity I envelop her in a hug from behind and kiss her back.

I feel her tremble beneath me, moving her around my heart constricts with pain seeing her tear stricken face. She looked dazed, her eyes are swollen, gently, I ask her "What happened, Naina?"

She gives me a blank look, which scares me off, as if she has to remind herself who am I, I could clearly see the display of emotions in her eyes, saying a word, "Dhruv" she puts her arms around me and held onto me tightly.

I am confused, I have never heard this name before, I have met all her friends but this name does not ring a bell. May be a distant relative, but the way she was crying it feels like she is very close to him, then why have I not heard this name. Giving her the comfort she needs, I wait patiently for her to stop crying. Pushing her back I made her sit on the sofa, give her a glass of water, I nudge her to speak further.

When she peaks again, she is avoiding my gaze, something is wrong, terribly wrong, "Dhruv … ummm.. he is the one I loved." Oh Shit …. What! I could not form any words, I calm myself down by telling myself she loved the person, it's her ex. One second why are we talking about him and why is she crying over him, maintaining my calm I nod to her, when I realise she is waiting for me to speak something.

She continues, "He has brain tumour, last stage. I am leaving tomorrow morning to meet him." I am just nodding stupidly to everything she is saying, I have never asked Naina about her past relationship as it never mattered and I never thought it will come back to haunt us. I am waiting for her to explain further, my all hopes vanish when she gets up and walks towards our room. I am sitting here contemplating what to do next. Times like this I really want to know what is going through her head. She looks so desolate and I fail to reach out to her. I know this is not the time my mind is pestering me to ask her what does this mean for us, how much importance do I have in her life.

Irritated with myself and my thoughts I get up to look out for some answers from Naina as I turn around I found her near the kitchen top with huge suitcase beside her. Raising my eyebrow, I silently question her, "I need sometime Nihal, I will call you once I know how he is." Saying this she walked away. I stood there motionless, deciphering what the hell just happened. I was fuming with anger, I wanted to bring her back and keep her locked down in our room, till I have all my answers. Raking my hands through my hair I threw all the culinary on the floor. My heart was fighting with me telling me to give her some time but my mind was fuming with anger, for once I want her to come up to me and talk to me. Kicking the table, I stormed into my room, I am tired, I need to sleep before I turn around and drag her back to this house.

CHAPTER 26

"What the hell, I asked for contract papers Andrew", I shouted at my PA.

"Sorry sir, I will just get them." Andrew fumbled with the files, while closing the door.

Raking my hands through my hair, I pushed the chair I was sitting on and walked towards the window. It's been two days since Naina went to visit Dhruv in the hospital, all I got was the message that she has reached. There has been no call or message after that. I am still angry with her for zoning me out of her life. I am supposed to be the support system in her life, the person she should fall upon in times of need. Looking up at the sky, I am remembering the last two months of our relationship; I thought we are moving forward, I thought I am as important to her as she is to me.

Standing here in my office, I feel I am back to the time when I met her for the first time, I feel I am still fighting for what is mine and I am still standing alone waiting for her to trust me. These two days without her have been really difficult; I miss her voice, her smile and her hugs. Blinking the moisture in my eyes, I realise I love her. I cannot afford to lose her for some loser who does not even care for her. It's suffocating not knowing how to reach the person you love so much. I know it would take me seconds to message her and know where she is but this time I am waiting for her to reach out to me. I know I am not a patient person at all, every hour without her call or message makes my blood boil thinking she does not need me as much I need her.

Before more doubts could creep in, my mobile beeps with a message, "How are you?" my lips twitch in a smile, my heart beats faster, my body relaxes, my love grows more when my silent question is answered, *"she needs me as much as I need her"*.

NAINA

I am trembling as I step out of the taxi towards the hospital, I hate hospitals, as I move further in towards the reception, I wish Nihal was there standing by my side. I enquired at the reception, "Dhruv, brain tumour patient, which room is he in?"

The nurse looked pissed, asked me to walk towards the first floor and second room on the left. Standing outside of the room, I am sweating profusely, I have not met him since we broke up at the café, my heart is begging me to knock the door and barge in but my mind is yelling at me to turn around and run before I draw myself into more mess than I am already in.

I almost turned around and was ready to run, when a doctor approached me, stopping me in my steps, "Are you here to see Mr. Dhruv?" Before I could stop myself I nodded, turning around doctor opened the door, ushering me in. Stumbling in I was greeted with the most painful sight, the person laying on bed had pale skin, there were wires attached to his arms, he was bald and it felt as if air has been sucked out of his body. Moving closer, I realised it was not the same Dhruv I loved, that one was handsome and well-built the person laying in front of me was nothing compared to the one I left behind.

Adjusting his bed, doctor called out to him, "Good Morning, Mr. Dhruv, how are you feeling?" My eyes are moving between him and the doctor, seriously is the doctor blind? Can't he see he is dying over here. Dhruv slowly opened his eyes, a smile hovering on his lips, "I am fine doctor". After responding he goes back to his peaceful state, doctor starts checking his vitals, I am standing there awkwardly thinking am I intruding something. I clear my throat thinking doctor will take a clue and introduce me, before he can introduce the same raspy voice spoke again, "You came". I looked around the doctor to see soulless eyes looking at me with shock and relief in them. Gaining some confidence, I spoke,

"Wasn't I supposed to?" I was confused, isn't that what he told me on phone, he wants to see me.

Smiling a little, Dhruv said, "Only you can combine humour with sarcasm." I am filled with mixed emotions, as I am angry for him contacting me after an year and dropping this news on me. Also I am sad because no matter how much pain he has caused me, I still would not wish anything this bad for him. Standing there clueless, convincing myself of one valid reason as to why I am here, I look up to see that Dhruv has again passed out. Putting a reassuring hand on my shoulder, doctor says, "He is in a lot of pain, his body cannot endure this pain, so he seldom passes out due this." I nodded again.

Nudging me forward, doctor asks me to follow him, dazedly I follow him to his cabin, gesturing to sit, he speaks, "So you are . . . ."

"I am his ex", I stare blankly. Nodding he continues, "Are you still in love with him?" His question jolted me out of my thoughts, am I still in love with him. Closing my eyes, leaning back in chair, I thought of the time the first time I saw him, instantly our three years flashed in front of me and I could only wince in pain remembering them. Before I could answer, doctor continues, "Sorry, I should not ask you personal questions. I only wanted to know your relationship with the patient."

"What happened to him?", I asked when doctor kept on looking at me. Sighing he told me, "Dhruv came to me six months ago, with the complaint of severe headaches and occasional blackouts. We kept him on some medications for some time but it worsened his conditions. After several tests it confirmed that he was on last stage brain tumour." Swallowing the lump in my throat, I asked him the question, dreading the answer already, "So how much time is left with him?"

Raising an eyebrow, he continues "A month or maybe 15 days, his body has stopped responding to our treatment. The tumour is fast spreading all over his body." I nodded again. I asked the only question that came to my mind after hearing all this, "When will he be awake again?"

"I have given him pain killers, so I am hoping he will be awake after two hours or so." I nodded, I realised nodding is what I have mastered in since I have come here. Looking with concern at me doctor said, "If you want you can wait in his room or we have a waiting lounge in every floor."

Clearing his throat, doctor continued, "I think you must be very special, because he has not informed anybody about his condition except for you." I stare blankly, feeling all the more confused. With a polite smile I leave his cabin and walk straight towards the waiting lounge. I don't have courage to sit in the same room when my mind is bombarded with so many questions inside.

It's been three hours I am waiting for the nurse to inform me if Dhruv has woken up. After few more minutes my name is called and I am ushered to his room. This time when I enter his room I am prepared to see him and ready with questions hovering in my mind. Looking up his eyes met mine and he smiled, I smiled back. It is awkward, what should I say *Hey, how are you, it's been long or Why the hell did you call me*. I stand there waiting for him to start the conversation because, seriously, I think I may start screaming at him if I am given the chance to speak.

Sighing, he signals me to sit down I look around for a chair and pull it towards his bed.

Exhaling slow breaths, he started, "How are you?" I look at him, thinking –really you want to know-- to which he smiled and continued, "I am sorry Naina. I really did love you but I am sorry. When I came to know about this tumour, all I have been thinking was to apologise to you." He started coughing in between, I got up from my seat and handed him a glass of water, I could see even little talking is taking a toll on his body. He continues, after sipping the water, "You were right for me, but I cannot commit myself to one. I wanted to apologise for all the bad I did to you". Looking straight into my eyes, with a pleading expression, he continued, "Can you forgive me?"

A tear escaped my eyes, as I listened to his apology which I have waited for a year. I got up from my chair and ran outside the room. I could not stop myself from crying. I still cannot bring myself to forgive him. This is the most difficult thing he is asking for from me. Sitting in the waiting room, I cried myself to sleep. A tap on my shoulder woke me up, I look up to find Dhruv's doctor standing in front of me, smiling with a cup of coffee. Embarrassed I sit up taking the cup of coffee from his hand. He sat beside me and we silently sipped the coffee, the warm liquid relaxing my body. After few minutes, doctor asked me, "If you don't mind, can I ask you a question?" I nodded silently sipping the coffee and savouring its taste.

"Why are you here?" this is the same question I have been asking myself since I entered the hospital. Shrugging, I answered, "I don't know". Nodding, we continued drinking our coffee's both lost in our thoughts. Then I saw him standing from his seat, he started walking out, at the exit he turned around and informed me, "You know you can stay with the patient in his room, one person is allowed to stay with the patient. Also I have given him the medication so he won't be waking up in the night at all." I nodded and gave him a smile.

Finishing my coffee, I strode towards Dhruv's room, I stood there looking at him, I realised I don't feel any anger for him, all I feel is sad. I make way towards the empty bed, while making myself comfortable, waiting for sleep to take over, only one thought remained in my mind, I miss Nihal by my side.

<h1 style="text-align:center">CHAPTER 27</h1>

Nihal

I am waiting outside the airport for my car to pick me up. The moment I got message from Naina telling me about her whereabouts without wasting anytime I booked my tickets for the next flight available. I handed the luggage to my driver and started looking for directions on the google maps. It would take me half an hour to reach the hospital, where Naina is. I am worried about her, it's the first time she has expressed her feelings to me. Opening my messages, I scroll down to the last one she has sent me yesterday night, "*Nihal, I need you. If it's possible can you come here, I need you around me.*" I was shocked and escalated both at the same time, I still have not replied to her message; I thought I would give her a surprise.

My driver informed me that we have reached the hospital I sprinted out of the car, making my way straight to the reception, "I am looking for Mr. Dhruv. What is his room number?" The nurse looked at me, checking me, battling her eyelashes, she then gave me the information. Smiling politely, I left for the room. Inhaling deep breaths, I opened the room, to find Naina holding hands of the person laying on the bed. An emotion so strong filled my whole body, then I looked around the bed, the sight in front of me was disheartening. A similar scene flashed across my mind, when I was young and my mom laying on the bed, helpless. Shaking my head, I moved across the room tapping on her shoulder.

Drowsy eyes met mine, first there was surprise and then they were filled with relief, as if I was the anchor she was holding on to. Instantly she got up from her seat and hugged me tight. It was the moment I realised though we have not voiced our love for each other but it is there in our actions. I hugged her back, tipping her head back I brought my lips over hers. I know this is not the right place or time but I needed her taste to fill up my senses. The moment she responded, I forgot everything and deepened the kiss. Somebody clearing their throat brought us back to reality, reluctantly I detangle myself from her.

I looked around at the person smiling fondly at us, I heard a timid voice of Naina from behind me, "Ummm... Good Morning Doctor". I spun around and looked again, doctor was directly looking at Naina while she was blushing red. What the hell! Why is he smiling at Naina so fondly, pushing her behind me, I glared at the doctor. Don't judge me I am possessive by nature and controlling too. Doctor gave me a polite smile and continued with his daily routine. Nudging me from behind, Naina motioned me to move out of the room.

Moving out, she held my hand and took me to a corner, where we could be alone for some time. Sighing she tugged me to sit and leaned her back against my chest. I was a little taken aback by her behaviour; it's always me initiating the closeness in our relationship. Tugging at her waist I pulled her closer believe me it feels like home when she is around. I don't remember how long we sat there because I think I dozed off. Next thing I know, Naina kissing my cheeks and waking me up from the uncomfortable position I was in. Looking around I smiled sheepishly at her, realising I slept for six hours straight. Not my fault I have not been able to sleep properly since she left me. I am used to sleeping beside her.

"Come on, wake up. Let's go somewhere to eat, I am hungry." Getting up from the chair, damn it was very uncomfortable, my back hurts I nod and follow her out.

As we were waiting for my driver, I saw Naina fidgeting with her fingers. A sure sign she is nervous, stretching myself I told her, "Let's go to my hotel room, we can freshen up there and order something to eat too." Looking into my eyes deep in thought she nodded. Before I could ask her what's worrying her, our car came. The drive to hotel was quiet, something was definitely bothering her, to make her relax I took her hands in mine, held them tight. Sighing, she relaxed leaning into me.

Silently we got out of the car when we reached hotel, I took keys from the reception guiding us towards the lift. Glancing sideways I saw her in deep thought, gliding my hand around her waist I pulled her in close proximity. I whispered in her ears, "Are you okay?" Faking a smile she said, "Yeah, I think so." I am still clueless what happened with her these past two days, what is she holding back and most of all will this impact our relationship. I have come to terms with my feeling that I love her and I am fighting for us but will Naina fight for us. The bell of the elevator startled me out of my worried thoughts, guiding towards our room, I pushed her in.

She is still walking in a daze, fidgeting with her hands, I decide to give her some time before I pound her with my questions, then I said, "I think I will go ahead, freshen up and you can order something for us." Nodding, she still stood in the room. Sighing I hand her the phone and in-room dining menu, raising my eyebrow, I command, "Order, Naina." Opening the menu, she starts going through it, and I moved in the bathroom.

Half an hour later when I emerged from the bathroom to see her sitting in front of the food she has ordered, smiling towards me she started laying the plates, moving slowly towards her, I grab hold of her chin and place a chaste kiss on her lips. Moaning she kisses me back slowly, I move back look into her unsure eyes and give her my best smile. I am unable to understand the awkwardness which has crept in between us. Naina, I know would blurt out the things troubling her but Niana, in front of me is hiding herself behind fake smile and regular nodding.

Just to make her at ease, I start with the conversation, "So…grilled cheese sandwich?" she nods. Taking my seat beside her, I continue, "Can you pass me the ketchup?", she nods again. Frowning I ask, "You know I eat a lot, hope you have ordered something else too." She nods. Frustrated, I turn her face towards me, I say slowly, "Naina, if you nod one more time instead of speaking, I sure am going to pin you to bed and have my way with you." Shocked she look into my eyes, shaking her head, she finally speaks, "Let's eat first, then I need to tell you something." Oh Shit! I have suddenly lost all my appetite; somehow I swallow the sandwich in front of me.

When we finished eating, in silence again, I saw her getting up and coming towards me, tugging at my hand she makes us move towards the bed. Clearing my thoughts, I said, "I mean seriously, if that's what you wanted, you should have told me I would have been more than happy to oblige." Turning around she glares at me then suddenly her lips twitch in a wide grin, shaking her head she says, "Nihal only you can make such sex innuendos in this situation and make me smile." My heart swells up with her compliment, I retort back, faking a gasp, "I was serious", to this she laughed, I could see her body relaxing. Tiptoeing on her toes she pecks my lips, shyly she says, "This is all that you are getting for now." She pulls me down the bed, makes herself comfortable between my legs her back pressing against my chest. Mind you this is our favourite position whenever we want to discuss or need comfort from each other. Sliding her hair away from her neck, I place soft kisses, I say, "What is bothering you, Naina?" groaning she leans back, making herself comfortable, she says, "Nihal I want to tell you a story and want you to listen it patiently." I nodded. Holding my hand at her waist, linking her fingers through mine, she starts, "There was this girl, who believed in love and waited for that love to sweep her away. Then one fine day, her prince charming came, that's what she thought, he treated her like a princess, gave her gifts, took her to places she was not aware of, cherished her in every way possible. The girl could not stop herself from falling in love with him. As time passed the prince changed, he started finding faults in the girl he called her love suffocating and accused her parents of controlling her. He started playing mind games with her and made her friends go against her. He hated her for her looks, her dressing sense and her being way too much emotional. The girl tried very hard to change herself for him, she stopped talking to the friends he disliked, she fought with her parents for him, she even started behaving the way he wanted, still it was not enough for the prince." A tear escaped her eyes and I slowly wiped it off. I pulled her closer if that was possible.

"Gradually the girl stopped smiling, lost her zeal towards life, was in constant fear of making him angry because if he gets upset he would lash out on her with cruel words and would insult her in front of her friends. Sometimes he would use her physically to satisfy himself but would never satisfy the girl. With each passing day the prince became colder towards the girl, leaving her with no option but to sulk and criticise herself. The time came when the girl lost all hope in her and succumbed to depression. Each day when she would get up, she would plaster a fake smile on her face for her parents but inside she was broken. The last straw broke when she found he was cheating on her. When the girl confronted him, he told her she was not able to satisfy him physically and emotionally. He told her she is just means to the end. He also told her that her love suffocates people around her and that's what pushes them away." Tears kept flowing from her eyes and my heart constricted with her words. There was no doubt that it was her story and she is letting me in. I was fuming with anger for Dhruv, so I decided to keep quiet.

We kept quiet for several few minutes, till she controlled herself and started again, "The girl was afraid of herself and promised to never fall in love again until one day she met the most wonderful person. Slowly this new person, through his stubbornness, started being a part of the girl's life, filling her life with surprises and love." My heart started beating faster when she finished the line with love, so does it mean she loves me.

Clearing my mind, I listened to what she was saying, "She was happy and everything in her life was flourishing, her career as well as her personal life. For once she thought, maybe now she has found that peace she was looking for. Contended in her world, ignorant of the fact that past will claw its paws in her life again. She thought she has made peace with her past but it was not true, when her past called her back she was consumed with anger all over again. She was confused, but she made her way towards one person she hates the most in life. The condition in which she saw him, made her heart ache with it. As a human she felt pity for him other than that she could not feel anything for him."

Turning around she looked directly into my eyes and asked, "Now that awful person who ditched her, asked the girl to forgive him but she does not know what to do. She is afraid of forgiving him, she feels it is easier for him, she wants him to grovel, feel the pain she have gone through, does that make her sound evil." Unshed tears hover around her eyes.

I pull her closer to my chest and hug her tight. I understand her conflict, her emotions. I don't blame her for being this cold towards him, he deserves it. For the first time I understand why she keeps running away from me, why does she have trust issues and why can't she let me take care of her? She is a self-made girl emotionally and personally and I am proud of her. My love for her has increased ten folds knowing what she has been through and how she fought with herself to prove herself that she is more than what others think for her. I have always loved her for being so strong, care free and independent. I know it's time she knows that I love her for who she is.

Pulling her chin up, I force her to look in my eyes, wiping away the tears from cheeks, I pull her close placing my lips closer to her mouth, I remain like this for few more minutes before I tell her, "This girl is not evil, love. She is strong, confident, independent and a fighter. It is hard to rebuild yourself when she was being pushed away by the love of her life. She has the right to be angry, to be revengeful but is revenge what she really craves, she has to decide that." Tears keep on falling from her eyes, with a hoarse voice she asks, "What other options does she have?"

Smiling, I wipe the falling tears, tracing her lips with my thumb, as I do this she shudders, I look straight into her eyes and speak, "She has two options, not to forgive the awful person, as she names him, and continue her life with guilt or forgive him and give this new person a chance to fill her life with love and smiles."

Exhaling, between sobs she says, "You…(sob)….the girl… (sob)..Was me". Bringing her face closer, few inches between our lips, I say, "I know, love." She closes the gap between us, her kiss is urgent and desperate, I return them with same intensity. As much as I need her, she needs me with same intensity. Sliding my hands from her back, I start unbuttoning her top, gasping she does the same throwing my shirt behind her, groaning I bring our body closer, we both need this touch, we both need this closeness between us.

Changing our positions, I lay her down on the bed, her lips are swollen from my kisses, her eyes are glowing with desire, moving my lips towards her neck, I start exploring her body inch by inch. It feels as if we are doing for the first time, as if she giving me herself altogether and I want to make it worthwhile for both of us. As I go lower towards her abdomen, she pulls me back, "Nihal, please I want you inside me now". Looking into her desire filled eyes, I unbutton my jeans, then short and discard them away and she does the same, positioning myself in between her legs, I ask "Have you brought your pill along" she nods and I thrust hard in her. She screams on top her lung, I know she wants rough but I slow my pace after the first thrust. She grips my hips harder, pulling them down I whisper in her ears, "Shhh love, I want to make slow love to you. I want you to scream and feel the pressure with each time I am in you I want you to remember how special it is between us." Moaning she bit my shoulder hard and I knew it's going to be my way. I keep making slow love to her, every time bringing her to peak and then withdrawing, starting all over again. By the time we climax we both were exhausted and instantly fell asleep in each other arms.

CHAPTER 28

Naina

I woke up to the thunder sounds from outside rubbing my eyes I look up to find Nihal sleeping peacefully. A lock of hair is falling on his face, carefully I swipe it away and he definitely needs haircut. How did I get so lucky, I have no idea? The whole Dhruv episode shook me up a little, making me confused but now I know where I belong. Moving myself closer to him, I kiss his nose and whisper, "I love you", saying them out does make me feel better. I promise soon I will say it to the person too who holds my heart and protects it in his own way. Tracing his jaw I peck his lips one more time, last night was amazing and I cannot keep this feeling all to myself any more. Before I tell him I need to sort a few things out, shifting slowly I lift myself from the bed and walked towards bathroom to take shower. I look back at the sleeping form on the bed and thank God's above for making him a heavy sleeper. With him asleep can quietly sneak out of the room and make my much needed last trip to the hospital.

After shower I dress in my old clothes as I forgot my bag at the hospital, I write a note to Nihal telling him about my visit to the hospital and asking him to book our flight tickets for the evening. I also told him to message me the flight details and I will meet him directly at the airport. I need to do this alone, I need this closure in my life, Nihal have already done a lot for him and I can't keep on pushing things on him more. After tucking the note at the bedside, I plant a kiss on his forehead, promising myself nothing else will come between us anymore.

After waiting for half an hour for Dhruv to wake up at the hospital, finally the nurse called my name and ushered me in. Dhruv's bed was titled up, making him sit vertically. He looked more tired than yesterday; I think the medicines are not at all working on his condition. I sat beside his bed on the chair, looking at me with tired eyes, he spoke, "I have requested the doctor to delay the injections by twenty minutes." He coughs and holds up one finger, asking me to wait, after the dry cough and taking few long breaths, he continues, "I wanted these twenty minutes for you, please tell me you have forgiven me."

I lean back in my chair and look at him, I know he is nervous his eyes are genuinely pleading me to forgive him, I still need to speak things to him before I relieve him from this suspense, looking straight into his eyes, I speak, "Dhruv I understand you need my forgiveness but before that I want to ask you, if you wouldn't have been diagnosed with this ill-fated disease, would you have come up and apologised for what you did." He was silent he kept opening and closing his mouth, I got my answers, I continued, "Never mind Dhruv, I always deserved much better in my life and finally I have got him. I am still recovering from the pain and hurt you induced upon me but I have come far from that and I know the person I am with will fill up all the holes in my heart with his love and care. Since, I am lucky enough to find my love and peace with him, I have decided to forgive you. I am not forgiving you because you asked me to, I am forgiving you because some wise person gave two options in life and I am choosing the option which will make me happy and loved." Finishing my great speech, I got up from my seat and started to leave from the room. Before exiting I look back and I saw thankfulness in his eyes. Satisfied I left the room and marched towards my last stop.

It's been over two hours I am waiting in the room, I have my flight in another three hours, I need to leave for airport in five minutes and I have no idea how much long will it take for him to complete the rounds. Just in case, if I miss the doctor I have already written the note explaining him everything. Looking at the watch, I got from my seat to leave and collided into the hard frame. Stumbling back, I peered up to see the smiling face of the doctor, finally. He raises his eyebrow in question and asks, "How come I became lucky, a beautiful lady waiting in my room."

Smiling and shaking my head, I handed envelop to doctor, frowning he looked up, I explain, "Doctor here is some money, I want to give for Dhruv's treatment, I know he must be using his insurance policy but please keep it, in case of emergency." Doctor nods, I continue, "A request doctor, whatever he needed from me I have given him, please do not contact me when the time is over. I am starting a new life and I want my past to cast its glow." I keep my head bowed as I cannot look into the doctor's intense gaze. I know I am being selfish not there for Dhruv when he needs me but I cannot handle this anymore, I have my life and I don't want to waste any time apart from Nihal.

When doctor does not say anything, taking it as my cue, I start to leave, when I reached the door, doctor says, "Thank you Naina for showing up for him. Since you have shown I have seen Dhruv happier and prepared for whatever is coming in his way." Turning around I see him smiling, seeing my eyes wide, he continues, "You seem shocked, I understand Naina how much hard it is for you", smiling sheepishly, he continues, "I heard your last conversation with him and I am glad to know you are much stronger than your emotions or feelings. You deserve to be happy."

His words made rid of the pending guilt I was harbouring in my mind. Smiling widely I thanked doctor for his words and left hospital with a light heart.

When I reached the airport just in time to board the flight, I hugged Nihal tightly thanking in my own way for all his support throughout, smiling widely, I say "Thank you". Kissing me on the forehead, he said, "Anything for you, beautiful. Anything for this beautiful smile, which rocks my world." Giggling I make way to the plane, knowing this where I belong. On the whole way back in flight I told Nihal everything that happened at the hospital including the money and doctor's wise words. He only asked one thing, after I told him everything, "Are you happy, beautiful" I smile and nodded. "That's what is important." I snuggle close to him and fall asleep.

Reaching back to Mumbai, I switched on my phone and saw 10 missed calls from Riya. I instantly called her back, she picked my phone on the second ring and shouted back, "Where the hell are you?"

Smiling, I replied, "Back from hell to heaven."

"Huh!"

"Nothing, what happened?"

"Well, I don't care wherever you are just get your crazy ass to my apartment now."

"Okay … But why?"

"Seriously, Naina, don't you remember we have to plan for Nimish's surprise birthday."

Oh! Shit! In all the drama in my life I totally forgot about his birthday, I reply, "I will be there in an hour." Looking up I see Nihal giving me a weird look.

"You better me and ask your lover boy to leave you alone for some time." Giggling she disconnects the phone, leaving me with wide smile and frowning Greek God.

CHAPTER 29

Naina

After a lot of pleading from myside Nihal left me at Ria's house. I wanted to confess my feelings to Nihal but then I never got the chance and I am scared now. though I now in my heart that he loves me, still there is one percent of me who thinks what if he needs more time. What if I am being too pushy about this? What if …

 "Where are you lost girl?" Riya nudged me. As we are planning a surprise for Nimish, we are staying at Riya's apartment. It's a small gathering, we wanted to make it special for him, the youngest in our group and everyone dotes on him.

Sighing I replied "Nothing, just lots going on in my mind."

"What's wrong, are you and Nihal having a fight."

"Nope nothing like that. It's just that I am being emotional, I guess."

"Spill it out girl." I told her about my visit to the hospital and then about morning, I felt so relieved telling her about all this.

"Okay. First of all, I am angry that you went to see that asshole but knowing you I know you needed that closure. Secondly, suck it up, everyone here knows how madly in love are you two for each other, its suffocating. Don't worry he is totally whipped girl." Riya gives me a wink and envelops me in hug.

"I am scared, what if he says no." I took the glass of coke from the table, hiding my nervousness behind it.

Riya gives me an exasperated look, "Seriously, Naina, you know what, go and talk to your lover boy. I think you are suffering from distance phobia syndrome." Laughing I look up from my glass into Riya's eyes, "Is that even a word, Riya."

"Of course not but I am inventing this for you. Now go and call him, I am sure he must be going nuts since you have not called him since morning."

Smiling I dialled him, after three rings, his calm voice fills my phone "Hi beautiful, how you doing?"

"Good. What are you doing? I did not have a call or message from your side the whole day."

Sighing into the phone, he speaks, "I thought you needed some time with your friends, though I was missing you a lot."

Smile appeared on my face, "I missed you too".

"Come home beautiful. I am craving for my sleep and it is difficult without you."

"I know me too. Nihal, I wanted to tell you something."

"Hmmm"

"Not on phone. Are you coming to Nimish's Birthday party tomorrow?"

There was a pause, "I am trying, beautiful, but please don't get angry if I don't make it."

I understand, his business is taking a lot from him, nodding I say "Of course, I understand. I will miss you." I meant it.

"I miss you too, love. I wish you were home tonight. I need you." For a minute I think of making an excuse but I know how important tomorrow is for every one of us.

"I wish too. Good Night." Though I wanted to say I love you but I wanted to say it face to face.

"Good Night, beautiful"

I pressed the red button a voice in me scolded me for being foolish. I decided I will tell Nihal I love him, I can't keep it inside me anymore. I needed to confess, I would do it tomorrow after Nimish Birthday party.

Nihal

After our short call I was confirmed Naina, was missing me a lot. Tomorrow I am going to make Naina mine forever. I have waited enough, I know I love her and I needed to tell her, make officially mine. Tomorrow Naina, after tomorrow I will keep you locked down in my heart forever. With that thought I slept with a huge smile on my face.

Today, is the most important day in my life, I was thankful to Nimish girlfriend for helping me in my plan. Yesterday, I spent most of my day at Jewellers finding out the most exclusive ring for her. I want to make it special for her and wanted it to be in front of the people she loves the most. I was happy Nimish birthday party was a small affair with all the close friends invited. Nothing could be more perfect than to propose her in front of everyone.

One hour more and then we will be together forever. I am wearing her favourite colour shirt and tie which she gifted me. I am nervous it's my first time I am proposing someone. Though I know she will not say no, still I am worried about her reaction. I gather the flowers, ring from the bed. I practice my speech once more in front of the mirror, I just hope everything falls the way I want.

I purposely delayed my entry at Nimish's Birthday, I wanted Nimish to enjoy his birthday surprise before meddling his day with my plans. I did not want the attention shift to our direction but then I couldn't have found a better day to propose her. Actually, I cannot wait one more day to be away from her. The party is at rooftop of the Sapphire Hotel, as I enter I recognise each of the faces present there. With time Naina friends have become my friends too. My eyes are still searching, it was then I saw a pink dress flowing, a face upturned towards the sky, as if she is thanking the universe for this beautiful day, which she often does when she thinks no one is watching her. She looks ravishingly beautiful, her make up as usual is minimum, wearing my favourite stilettoes, the dress is showing off her perfect legs, it's an off shoulder dress, all I want is to run my tongue across her shoulder, kiss her neck, bite her ears, then suddenly as if sensing I am here, she looks in my direction.

First she seems shock, shakes her head and then a smile stretches across her beautiful face so wide that my heartbeat doubles its moment in that minute. Standing there like an idiot gaping at my girlfriend soon to be wife, I snap myself out of my reverie and starts walking towards her. Meeting her in the middle I envelop her into a hug, smiling she whispers "I missed you, Handsome."

Pulling myself back I kiss her on the lips, I missed her too. As if realising where we are, she pulls herself away from the kiss, smiling sheepishly she looks around and give me a glare. I could not stop myself from grinning this is the girl which makes my world filled with happiness and love. Taking of hold of my hand, she started pulling me towards the birthday boy, I stood there turn her around with the same hand and mouthed her to stay.

Confused she looked at me, taking a step back, keeping her eyes locked with mine, I slowly bent down on one knee. I kissed her hand and spoke looking directly into her eyes "When I first saw you, I couldn't take my eyes off you. I was lost in your eyes and smile. Your smile fills up my whole world there isn't a day I would like to spend without you. Since you have been so adamant to not move in with me and I am hopelessly in love with you, want to keep you by my side always. I am asking you, Naina will you marry me and fill up my life with your constant presence, love and warmth always."

By the time I finished, I could see tears rolling down her cheeks, then she started laughing, I thought she was having a panic attack. You see with Naina you have to expect the worst because she will never react the normal way a person should react in a situation. I raised an eyebrow to her reaction, as I felt a little awkward kneeling down when she was laughing uncontrollably. What seemed like an eternity she bend down, pulled me in for a kiss which went a little too long, whispering "Yes, I Iove you too" between kisses. I dragged her up, kissed her hard one last time and slipped the ring on her finger "I love you, beautiful."

EPILOGUE

Looking in the mirror, I admire the bridal lehnga I am wearing. It is a beautiful combination of pink, green and red that matches the jewellery I am wearing. My mom standing behind me, I could see tears rolling down I know she is very happy. Finally, I am getting married, though I took my own time for this day to arrive.

After Nihal's grand proposal, I have been on cloud nine. I heard, read about fairy tales, never knew my life would turn out into one. Meeting him was very accidental, when I look back to the previous year, how universe planned to give me my happily ever after, which I thought would be never happen. Standing near the window, looking out the vast expanse of the farmhouse I am very grateful to the God's above, for bringing Nihal in my life.

After a month from the proposal, Nihal is work schedule became a little more bearable, I took him to meet my parents. Though knowing my mom it was difficult to believe she would give any hard time to Nihal. OMG! She interrogated Nihal through and through, about his business, his sex life (Well! That was one hell of an embarrassing situation), thankfully I gave Nihal heads up before making him meet my crazy family. It was only that two hours of grilling initially, other than that everyone have loved Nihal to the core. Seeing now how Nihal and mom have ganged up against me, will make it hard to believe the initial grilling session. My mom only kept one clause in front of Nihal before she could say yes, that I am supposed to visit them once in every month, though it started with fifteen days but knowing Nihal it was difficult to strike a bargain that hard. Finally, they agreed for once a month.

Looking up at the universe, I am questioning how I got so lucky to have filled my life with so much love. Nihal's dad is a very pleasant man, the moment Nihal introduced me to him, he enveloped me into a hug and have been calling me his daughter since then. If Nihal has my mom, I have his dad (it is a win-win situation). Happy and content are the two words filled in the dictionary of my life. We did not fix the date immediately I convinced Nihal that we should give ourselves a year before getting married, Oh! I tell you it was not easy, it required lots of arguing and make up sex but finally he agreed.

Nope, it was not that I was afraid I just needed time to settle things for me. Past three months have stayed with my family I left my job and fully concentrated on myself. Of course, Nihal was not happy with my decision, God he even suggested dad to move to Mumbai and settle here. It was difficult to stay away from him but I needed my family around me. Nihal would not agree but being separate have made our love stronger.

Mom touched my shoulders making me jump, nervously I turn around, aske her "How do I look?"

"The most beautiful bride I have ever seen". My mom smiling face and reassuring eyes, made my body relax.

"Naina, it's time. Let's go and meet your bridegroom." Rolling my eyes and smiling widely, I lead the way.

Outside the room, my friends are waiting for me, giggling and giving me compliments they accompany me to the garden outside, where my blue-eyed Greek God is waiting for me. We are getting married at Nihal's farmhouse, it exactly the way I wanted, out of the city, with only family and friends around. I remember, before moving back to my parents I spent the last night at Nihal's place, after an intimate and wild sex he asked me how I want our wedding to be. Casually I told him I want a small affair with friends and family in a farmhouse. The whole farmhouse to be covered with orchids, roses and lilies. In the centre of the farmhouse, I want the Mandap to be in same shade of colour as our dresses. The path to Mandap to be filled with roses with a soft music playing when I enter the garden.

As I step outside the garden, that is exactly I found, my face was a mask of surprise when I saw the whole setting, it was exactly what I wanted. Each & every detail has been carefully looked up on I could not stop the tear rolling down my left cheek. It felt like I was entering a fairy tale wedding. looking straight I found Nihal standing in front of the Mandap waiting for me, my heartbeat escalated, exhaling heavy breaths, slowly walking the path (as instructed by the photographers), I came close to my going to be husband. I could see Nihal's eyes boring into me, I could not stop the smile on my face, for a moment I forgot I was surrounded with people, it was just my Greek God and me in our fairy tale wedding.

He brought his hand forward, I gave my hand in his and mouthed "Thank You", grinning he came forward and whispered, "I love you." Blushing, smiling I looked into his eyes. Kissing me on my cheeks, he said "You look gorgeous, Naina". It's the way he says it and my whole body relaxes, then lowering his voice making it more seductive "Can we skip the whole rituals" confused I look up, smiling wickedly he says "I can't wait to tear this dress, make you moan loudly, while I am thrusting hard into you." Shocked I look into his eyes, he cannot be serious, everyone is looking at us and here he is speaking filthy words into my ears making me wet. Before I could speak anything, Nihal tug at my hand and moved forward.

The whole time he kept smiling and winking at me. I shake my head clearing myself of all the lustful thoughts, concentrating on vows, which will bring us together forever and ever. I was waiting for the part after all the rituals get over I have surprise planned for Nihal. We were sitting at the dinner table with other guests, smiling and celebrating our togetherness. Quietly I excused myself and went over the stage, asking for everyone's attention, I looked up from the mic saw Nihal wearing a confused and surprised

expression, calming my nerves I said "Nihal, my husband, yeah
that sounds a little weird." I pause and look around everyone was
smiling waiting for me, I continued, "I love you, husband.
Thanking for this beautiful day, making me believe fairy tale exist.
You have given me everything, making me a happy bride, I wanted
to give you a part of me, I thought what better than expressing my
love for you in a poem. You my husband are very precious to me.
here I go"

It's not every day I feel alone

It's not every day I feel the missing

It's not every day I feel the emptiness

But sometimes yes I do.

Untainted love, wicked smile,

Twinkling eyes, stimulating kisses,

Something tells me it is a fairy-tale,

I am waiting for mine to tell.

Given chances, getting up hopes,

Taken a leap of faith,

Then breaking it into pieces,

Still waiting for my story to be made.

Looking into the eyes knowing it will stay,

Falling into arms knowing its forever,

Getting up to you knowing it isn't a phase,

Commitment that will never fade.

Looking back I admire the qualities I fell for,

Learnt at each step not having any regrets for,

Never lost faith in myself ever,

Found my love forever.

Not expecting it to be Romeo and Juliet,

Not expecting it to be epitome of love,

Only you and me in our little world,

Learning, loving and knowing each other,

The Should I's will not stop us for falling for each other.

Finishing the poem I directly looked into the eyes of only one person, the look he gave me was all I needed to know that my happily ever after is actually the beginning and not the end.